Walk On, Bright Boy

ADVANCE UNCORRECTED GALLEY

144 pp.   ISBN-13: 978-1-57962-153-7

ISBN-10: 1-57962-153-8

Pub. Date: August 2007 $26 cloth

Walk On, Bright Boy

a novel by

Charles Davis

THE PERMANENT PRESS

Sag Harbor, NY 11963

ISBN 13: 978-1-57962-153-7
ISBN 10: 1-57062-153-8

For the without whoms,
above all my parents
and Jeannette

ACKNOWLEDGMENTS

My thanks to Martin and Judith Shepard, publishers above and beyond the ordinary, and to everyone at The Permanent Press, in particular Gloria Pillow for her close reading of the text. The ideas behind this story were inspired by a lot of living and a lot of reading; amongst the latter, the most stimulating was Rebecca Solnit's magisterial history of walking, Wanderlust (Verso 2001).

My parents did not intend that I should learn letters, still less that I end my days confined and awaiting the pleasure of the Holy Spanish Inquisition. The confinement is perhaps a consequence of the letters, but I do not regret the learning that has brought me to this pass. Without words I would at best have become the factor for a monastery, laying it hard on tenants and counting the tithe on my tally stick, would in my own sense have been a man without language or favor. As regards my present situation, it is like the Moor said, no one throws stones on a tree without fruit.

The Moor was our *acequero*. My people knew nothing of the mountain, so one moor in each village was made to remain in order to maintain the *acequias* and show the Christian settlers how to irrigate the land. It was a thankless task, but the Moor was not a bitter man and whatever sorrow pricked his heart was never painted on his face. Walking the *acequias*, clearing the channels of rocks, shoring up the embankment, crawling along cliff faces where the canal was carved into the rock, he was as bright and sparkling as the water he brought to our crops, and we children loved him for it, for we needed his tricks and tales as our parents had needed his knowledge of irrigation when they arrived.

I still remember the terror of being a child. I do not mean the fear caused by incomprehension or ignorance, nor the dread of being punished or beaten, but the terror of being taken. Children disappeared, you see. Every once in a while, one would go missing. And though the villagers searched the riverbeds and the wells and the caves and the bottom of the *tajos*, no trace of the missing child was ever found. They just disappeared. And until my ninth year, this tax on youth was endured with the stoicism of despair. As the Inquisitor knew too well, a people who have been displaced want confidence in their tenure and, if whole populations could be moved by potentates, a mere child might be spirited away like chaff on the wind.

Then a baby died. On the whole, that is what babies did. I'm not talking about the disappeared, but the newborn, whose grasp on life was even more tenuous. Only the occasional child made it past the age of three. Infancy was so hazardous that survival itself might have been reckoned suspect, the achievement of adulthood virtual confirmation of some occult mischief. But in this instance, having lost three children in as many years, one among the disappeared but two months earlier, the distraught mother claimed witchcraft. And once the cry was out, everyone was thinking about the year's poor crop, the scolding wife, the beating husband, the indolent son, the unkind father, the rats in the corn, the cold, the heat, the floods, the drought . . . in short, the miserable lot of a benighted people was not that, not what it was, not normal in a disrupted community transplanted to a place not of its own making, but something that might be blamed on an external agent, and so resolved if only the agent were identified. People love to ascribe blame. It makes life so much easier. And if they could have witches in the town, why not in the country, where the cross was so much thinner on the ground? Not literally, of course. Literally it was everywhere, daubed on the walls and along the paths, proclaiming our fragile victory. But figuratively, ours was barely a Christian land and the painted crosses faded fast in that harsh climate.

Our priest was a poor illiterate man, scraping a precarious subsistence from the soil like the rest of us. With hindsight, I realize he knew nothing of the liturgy, but had learned a miscellany of Latin phrases which he scattered about his services more or less at random, filling the gaps with a mumbo-jumbo of his own making. If he represented God in the *aldea*, doubtless the Devil was having a very gay time of it indeed. So when the cry of witchcraft was raised, he was helpless and outside authority was required—someone with the wherewithal to assign blame and mete out punishment.

* * *

We children had never seen such a personage as the Inquisitor. When first he rode into the village, astride his fine horse and dressed in his rich clothing, we fled in fear, for surely such a gorgeously caparisoned figure could be none other than God or the Devil himself, and given the hue and cry we had heard of late, nobody was waiting for God in that place. Our priest evidently had his doubts, too, for though he did not flee, his diffidence was manifest. As I peered from behind a hayrick, I saw him pushed forward to greet our august visitor, and I suspect several among the villagers, not least those who had been most clamorous for just such a progress, were beginning to regret their calls for an inquiry. There was no telling what would happen with such a grand figure as that brought among our sorry community.

As it transpired, the presence of the Inquisitor had little to do with the supernatural fears of a few credulous peasants. Sorcery, I know, has never been a concern of yours, my lords. It is one of the few bright spots in your dark history that, while the rest of Christendom was crying witch, your inquiries dismissed most purportedly diabolic covenants as harmless female vaporings. Even had you cared for such matters, our miserable *aldea* would scarcely have merited the attention of a tribune, no matter how auxiliary he was in the gradations of your order. But with the late removal of the *moriscos*, the Inquisition was without its main source of income, the fines imposed on villages where forcibly baptized Moors, speaking no tongue but their own and having nothing but a few hastily translated phrases to bolster their new faith, were vulnerable to your charges. Short of both heretics and funds, the order was prepared to undertake missions that would previously have been deemed too mean for men puffed up with the pride of righteousness.

Of course, your moral purpose has always been marred by more worldly motives, deposing those you envy while ensuring that the crown maintains control of its disparate peoples, but in this instance the political end was of a different order. The Inquisitor's mission was one of diplomacy in a place where military success had outstripped the competence of settlers. The Moor understood this. He knew all about the frailty of victory. He always said the walker claims the land better than any army, for while the army merely subjugates a place, soaking it in blood, the walker becomes a part of the landscape, impregnating himself in it. The one is a stain, the other substance.

This walking is something for which I have always been grateful to the Moor. My people walked, too, going to the fields, taking the herds to the high pasture in summer, descending to sell or trade what little could be spared, but not like the Moor walked. He walked to live, it was his job: following the *acequias*, portioning out the water, walking back to the source, walking the life-giving liquid down the mountain. This is a grand, godly way of being—is it not?—treading the spring of life from source to fruit, gauging flow against need, and ensuring each receives the agreed number of gates. It was a life that would have suited me well, for the Moor infected me with a taste for walking, walking and talking, telling myself tales, so that the two activities came to resemble one another so closely,

I can no longer easily separate them. For me, a path is like a simple story and every time I walk, I am telling myself a tale of the world I traverse. Even now, I pace up and down my room dictating to my amanuensis . . . no, you will not find him here when you come. After that first betrayal, I vowed never to betray another again and, by my lights, it is a vow I have maintained. You will not find his identity here. Only the words he transcribes from my curious walking, talking progress.

The walking is relevant to my testament. You may well know of it already. I have gained a reputation during my days in office, a reputation that varies according to the quality of your cloth, for I am a holy fool to the poor and a perfidious radical to the rich. That reputation is due in part to walking. To see a man of my status on foot is at once a miracle and a scandal. Some among the poor previously misdoubted whether men of my ilk had legs to walk on, while wealthy prelates fear I am like to start preaching a poverty they have never known nor wish to learn. Even as I approached my allotted span (long since expired, so your efforts can only conclude what should have been done a decade gone), I would descend from my carriage on some dusty road to walk alongside my retinue. It was a practice that caused exquisite agonies among my secretaries, for they could not let me, their superior, walk alone, yet believed it beneath their dignity to do likewise. And I learned it all from the Moor.

That was in part the cause of his denunciation. The Inquisitor wasted no time. He had no wish to remain among us longer than was necessary and took little pride in his appointed task. It was a job compelled by expediency that should be concluded with a comparable expediency. That same day, he summoned the first witnesses—the woman who had lost her child, the men who blamed their own fecklessness on a malign fate, and the parents of other children who had disappeared over the years, for they too saw in this occasion an opportunity to express a pain they had otherwise forgotten, to claim for themselves some small place in the gratifying pantheon of the victims. And who was to blame? The outsider, of course. It was the Moor they named, the Moor they blamed, for had he not stolen their children's hearts? It was only natural that he should be the one who had stolen their bodies, too, draining the children of a vitality he was in truth most responsible for stimulating in the first place. And by the time of which I speak, they knew enough to manage the *acequias* on their own. They did not care to keep among them the motif of their theft.

The Moor knew it was coming, too. He had told me before, ten peasants can sleep under one blanket, but two kinds won't fit in an entire country. For your benefit, my lords, as I doubt it is a distinction you would make unaided, he was speaking about the New Spain of Old Christians, where one of my kind, I regret to say, was responsible for construing virtue through the fractured vernacular of the statutes of *limpieza de sangre*. There is no pure blood, my lords, nor any tainted, only the blood some would shed and others preserve, the ink with which we proclaim our affinity for death or life. Set against your own narrowing notions, the Moor's maxim was descriptive, not prescriptive. He knew, all too well, what he was talking about. I hope the knowledge helped him, as my knowledge of what is to come and why it must be, helps me. A little.

* * *

Before his people were expelled, the Moor had been the village song-maker, though his song-making was by way of an avocation rather than a vocation. He worked his land and took his turn on the *acequias*, as did all the able-bodied men, but like many villages in those days, the *aldea* was used to have one among its number with a talent for telling tales, and whenever there was a notable event, it fell to the Moor to make a song of it, composing a kind of history of his people as he accumulated verses over the years. It was this talent that drew the children to him. He did not dare tell us of his own people, but, knowing the land, he would recount how the Two Sisters came to have their name, what drove mad the man immortalized in the Shepherd's Leap, the singularity of the Wolf's Cave, and whyfore the Giant's Steps. Coming new to this world, we children soon learned where to gather and what to ask to elicit a story, and were readily beguiled by his narrative of a foreign land that was all around us.

His gift for gaiety was one reason our elders resented him. They could not, in any event, have found it easy. He was an infidel, a man who was at home where they would be at home, but were intolerably uneasy, an outsider in number, but an insider in knowledge. To depend upon him had already caused hard feelings. But that his ease should be expressed in a talent for life they so clearly lacked was a provocation too far. Coming from the North, my own forebears were a thin rain-sodden milk-and-cider people whose sour native gloom was cruelly exposed by the bright light of the South, and their dour ways contrasted ill with the Moor's love of wine and laughter. That he should sing about it, too, was like bending to a crack in the door to spy on a celebration from which you were excluded and then receiving a poke in the eye for your troubles. And he had stolen their children, too.

I was too young when we arrived to trace our enchantment. Doubtless when first we came the children shared their parents' suspicions of the Moor and probably expressed their misgivings with the naked unkindness of their innocence. But by the time I was of an age to remember, whenever the Moor walked into the mountains, he would trail a flock of children behind him, all chattering and playing, roused from the dull dominion of their ordinary lives by the promise of discovery with which he invested every walk.

He was full of visual tricks, too. He would, for instance, fold the thumb of his right hand in his fist and hold the tip of the other thumb between the forefingers of his left hand, so that when he put his fists together, what appeared to be the end of his right thumb protruded from the forefingers of his left hand. Then he would call on us to pull his hands apart. After much grimacing and a great play of pain we knew to be play but thrilled to nonetheless, his hands would separate, apparently pulling the thumb off his right hand in the process, and only 'magic' would see the digit healed.

He also claimed to have an invisible 'sleepy-dust' that he would sprinkle on our eyes to make us doze off. He had big, dry, blunt-fingered hands, and when he rubbed a thumb against his fingertips it set up a soft rasping sound so that you could almost believe an infinitely light dust really was trickling into your eyes, and we would indeed sometimes doze off, entranced by the whisper of his fingers and the soft murmuring of his voice. And once he took us fishing for the moon.

I forget the season, but it was late enough for the days to be short and early enough for the snows not to have fallen. We were descending from the mountain—the Moor, myself, and two others. The moon was full and the path was clear and we could see the diffuse silhouette of the *aldea* swaddled in haze from the evening cooking fires. As we crossed middle brook, where the turbulent white water was bright with the light of the moon, the Moor told us about a young boy who had caught a fragment of the moon while fishing on just such a night as this. Seeing our puzzlement but sensing our willingness to suspend disbelief, he cut a branch from a coppice, and produced a length of yarn and a hook from his pack. Soon he was schooling us in the occult art of fishing for the moon.

Dangling his line in the dancing stream, he would suddenly flick a spray of glistening water into the air, yelling exultantly that he had caught a piece of the moon, only to look immeasurably forlorn when it fell away and disappeared in the deep coarse grass. Perhaps we, being nearer in age to the original fisherman of the moon, would have better luck? Before long we were all at it, turn and turn about, dabbing the hook in the reflected light in an attempt to catch some of its magic and mystery. I never really believed we were fishing for the moon, but neither was I wholly convinced we were not. That was a part of his talent, to move in us children irrational beliefs that enhanced life. Sadly, he also moved irrational beliefs in adults—beliefs or fears, they amount to the same thing.

I don't think there was any purposeful determination on the part the villagers to take revenge on one who had done no harm but be brighter than themselves, at least none that was spoken aloud. My parents, like the others, probably genuinely believed that the Moor was some mischievous sprite bewitching, then stealing their children, cursing their crops, causing their wells to collapse . . . whatever their particular grievance may have been. It was just that he was there and conveniently culpable. Only the Moor, myself, the Inquisitor, and one other knew for sure he was innocent of the charges leveled against him. It was unfortunate though that he should have walked on water. For that simple fact lent credence to every fanciful accusation my people made and gave the Inquisitor the pretext he needed.

* * *

I know now that the Inquisitor was a good man— or, at least, as good as any man may hope to be within the constraints of such a calling. He was not one of the breed that accuses simply to accumulate, for whom the wealth of the heretic is the defining sin (rest assured of my most worthy intentions, my lords), nor one so weak in his own faith he had to affirm it by asserting its superiority over the belief of others.

Yes, my lords, you read that sentence correctly. You may use it against me, too. I will sign this document. I willingly declare that the world is a circle with different paths leading to the center; there are three paths, each with a different perspective, but their object is the same. I hope that will save you some time and me some unpleasantness, though I fear you cannot appease an envious man who is dissatisfied with himself, so perhaps this voluntary confession will serve no purpose.

For his part, the Inquisitor was not a man who took pleasure in the implements of torture. His inquiries were not conducted by means of the *strappado* or the *aselli*. He might have tortured a confession from the Moor or sought repentance by similar means, but instead he chose trickery. It is a more appropriate weapon for political purposes, as you should well know, my lords. You pretend to be protecting the faith, but in truth yours is a political art playing a more subtle trick on the people, deploying fear and suspicion to counter disunity and disobedience.

I first met the Inquisitor on the patch of beaten earth that passed for a plaza in the *aldea*. The encounter took place under the old lime tree, which the Moor said had been planted a hundred years before and had lately constituted a kind of parliament for his people, being the place where they held public meetings, and where he had sung his songs of celebration and commemoration. Whether the Inquisitor chose that spot because it was at the heart of the village, or merely because it was the only convenient clean and cool location to shelter from the summer heat, I do not know, but in the time he was among us, he spent the greater part of the day sitting under that tree, and that was where he received most of the plaintiffs' depositions.

I was returning from the communal well, heavily loaded, and was concentrating on not spilling my burden, so I did not at first hear him calling me. My parents were too poor to have their own well, so fetching water, sometimes three times a day, was one of my main tasks as a child. In later years, having water brought to my rooms was one of the few luxuries I really enjoyed. You, who were born well and have never had to trouble yourselves with life's chores, cannot appreciate what such simple things signify for ordinary people, but water has always been important to me. I know what it means to have the hard wood of the yoke cutting into your neck and shoulders and the great weight of the laden leather buckets drilling shafts of cramp down the muscles of your back. Moreover, water was the matter of the Moor's life and, indirectly, his undoing. It is, for me, a kind of medium, by which I may compute my passage from poverty to high estate, and remember both the sporadic drama and daily tedium of my early years.

When the Inquisitor repeated his call, I could tell by the tone of his voice that it was not the first time he had spoken, for there was an impatience to his summons that reminded me of my mother when she caught me dreaming of some far away world conjured by the Moor's tales.

Dreaming is a strange word to use for one brought up in such circumstances. My people did not dream. They had neither the wit nor the leisure for dreaming; and anyone who submitted to fancy was supposed simple-minded if not actively, even malignantly, demented. It must have come as a terrible shock to them when I was taken away to be educated. The motives for my removal were complex. It was not simply a question of innate talent being recognized. I was removed to ensure that the truth was not revealed. But I think my capacity to dream was also, at least in part, responsible. And for that I had the Moor to thank. Listening to his tales, I learned that the mind is a landscape and that, just as we can walk across a hill to see what's on the other side, we can explore the world by walking through our minds. Doing some dull task like crushing almonds or shelling chestnuts, I would wander through my mind, and my movements would become slower and more mechanic, until eventually I was doing nothing visibly constructive and would receive a scolding from my mother, often as not followed by a cuff about the side of the head. Which is why I was brought up short by the way the Inquisitor spoke to me. I knew that voice. I knew I was being summoned to some less pleasant aspect of what adults took to be reality.

"You are of this village?" he said, as I approached the lime tree, having put down my load. It was an absurd question. Had I not been of that village, I would not have been staggering about with a brace of buckets hanging from my shoulders. But that was part of his technique, asking first what was redundant before inquiring, in much the same tone, about a matter of greater import.

I admitted that I was from the village, fearful that my confession would automatically entail some guilt. I did not at that time understand why he was there. I knew it had to do with the death of the child and the disappearance of others and with a hundred other woes that had until then seemed merely the normal lot of my people, but in what way this was to be resolved by the Inquisitor, I had no idea.

"You know the Moor then?" he said.

I barely dared reply, for though I knew the Moor and loved him dearly, I also knew this was not a knowledge one spoke to other adults. All the children understood that, veiling their exploits on the mountain with a silence that can only have exacerbated their parents' resentment. Yet, faced with that penetrating gaze and those fine clothes, I could not deny the man, so admitted that I did indeed know the Moor. The Inquisitor's next question was wholly unexpected.

He said: "What manner of man is he?"

It had never occurred to me before that there were 'manners' of men. I knew there were men I liked and men I disliked, those marked by kindness and those for whom the world was an unceasing source of spite to be responded to in kind, but that these should be 'manners of men' was a new concept. People just were, their characters fixed entities that one did not question. And yet I had the wit to reply. That, I think, was why the Inquisitor came to the solution he did when deciding what, eventually, was to be done with me. I nearly always had the wit to reply, a talent that helps explain my present predicament.

I said: "Please, your lordship, he is a good man."

I am glad I said that. And that I later repeated it in front of everyone. It didn't change anything. The Inquisitor probably didn't even hear it. It was only a simple statement of fact. But when one considers what happened afterwards, it is of some solace that I was at least consistent in my public opinion of the Moor.

"Are you one of the children who has followed him in the mountains?"

"Yes, your lordship. All the children do."

"Why do they follow him?"

"Because he tells us stories, your lordship."

"What manner of stories?"

Again that 'manner.' Were there manners of stories, too? This time my wit failed me.

"Does he tell you stories, for instance, about God?" he prompted.

"No, your lordship."

"Spirits, then. Sprites, creatures of the night, sorcerers, anything of that nature? Are the stories all different or do they in some way resemble one another?"

I was bewildered. Stories were a still pond reflecting the world. You did not try to look below the surface or say what they were about. If you did, the reflection blurred and the story lost its shape.

The Inquisitor wanted something specific, though.

He was perfectly still, watching me much as a lizard looks on a fly.

His stare was so intense I could feel my face grow warm.

"They're about here," I said, after a silence that seemed to have lasted several weeks. "About us and the mountain; he tells us stories about these things."

"That is why you follow him, for stories about the land?"

"Yes. . . ."

Sensing my hesitation, he said: "And. . . ."

It was a command, not a question.

"For the walking, your lordship."

This time he was the one momentarily at a loss.

"For the walking?" he said. I nodded. "You go with him for the walking?"

He did not ask for details, but he had understood. Walking was important.

My betrayal of the Moor was begun.

* * *

Walking is important. The Moor knew that. In the days immediately after the Inquisitor's arrival, the Moor was still at liberty. He must have seen what was happening, probably guessed its likely outcome, but he did not try to escape. He simply continued as he had before, walking and talking, talking and walking, as if the paths he walked were without end, the stories he told timeless.

You may not understand this matter of walking. Perhaps someone else will be sent, but I suspect I know the manner of man (I learned my lessons well) who will first read these words. Is your walking defined by anything less predictable than carpets, tiles, cloisters, and walls? When did you last walk further than the stable? Do you know any path other than the one that leads to your carriage door? Have your ever traveled a distance that was not covered on the back of a horse or on the deck of a boat? These things, moving by the grace of the elements or the labor of a beast, are not progress. They are merely a purchased transition. You buy your passage. That is the way we men of means orchestrate our living. Travel, shelter, food, they are all bought. We pay our way from birth to death. But if that's all you do, you have experienced little and understood less. All you have done is acquire the paltry trick of gathering a little comfort about your person.

Walking, by contrast, is hard. It is tiring, frequently uncomfortable, occasionally dangerous. But it cannot be bought or sold. We do not walk better for having a bigger purse. We are what we are, no more, no less, nothing lost for want of a coin, nothing gained for a piece of gold. As a result, when we walk, we measure ourselves against the world. And we see how small we are. Walking teaches that humility which you simulate in the face of God, but discard when dealing with men. Walking, we rediscover the limits of ourselves.

There is a story the Moor told me. A scholar embarked on a boat and asked the boatman if he had ever studied grammar. When the boatman said no, the scholar sneered at him, and said that half the boatman's life had been wasted. A storm blew up and the boat began to sink. Asked if he had ever learned to swim, the scholar said no. "Then your whole life is wasted," said the boatman, and dived into the sea to swim ashore. Like the supercilious scholar, the man who fails to walk, the man who has not measured himself against the world, has wasted his whole life.

This gauge is also the means by which we first assert our autonomy and has to be nurtured in later life lest the motivating instinct be wasted by the contrivances of ingenuity and indolence. An infant starts to walk in order to explore its world and get what it wants. That is to say, we walk to learn and to realize ourselves. Walking is therefore the corporeal expression of free will. If the gift of free will is not to wither away, if being itself is not to be reduced to mere existence, we must continue to walk throughout our adult lives, exploring, seeking, learning.

As a child, I did not realize how important walking was. I sensed that it was tied to storytelling, that the Moor measured his tales according to the pace he walked, just as I now meter my sentences by the confines of this room, but that the walking was a form of storytelling in itself, a way of finding your way through the world, that revelation came to me later, when my betrayal of the Moor had earned me an unexpected education.

Naturally, not every story, or every walk, will have a desirable end. When we hear a story or follow a path, we trace the route taken by someone in the past. The story or path does not necessarily lead us where we want to go. But they are each a way into the world, a way of experiencing things we have neither the wit nor the talent nor the time to experience otherwise. And if the path does not lead where we thought it might, no matter. It's how we get there that is important.

Do you understand this, you who do not move but on the back of something else? Maybe I do you a disservice. I recall from my reading that before the Moors were expelled, in the days when a *convivencia* was still sought, they were required to modify their behavior, including the way they walked. Maybe you and your kind do understand after all. Certainly, the Inquisitor appreciated that roaming the mountains constituted a liberty that was dangerous to authority. But in this matter I think even he lacked the finesse of the Moor, who knew there are different ways of walking for different people and different circumstances, and that how you walk may determine what becomes of you. That was one lesson of which I did not take proper heed.

Ship-ship was the phrase he used. Whenever we walked quietly, stalking some unsuspecting animal, creeping home after dark, stealthily approaching a stream to scoop a trout from the bed, he would smile and murmur *ship-ship*. It was intended to convey the small sound of our feet. But he also used it on another occasion, of which I will tell later, and then the movement was of no matter. It was discretion he was recommending, treading softly, for the world we walk in is not always well disposed to us. I never learned that discretion, which is why I await your arrival. But the rest of it, I did understand—eventually.

When the Inquisitor dismissed me, I hurried away as fast as the heavy buckets permitted. I had no sense of having done wrong, of having contributed to the Moor's downfall, and, in fairness to myself, what I had said until then was hardly damaging to him. Though I had taken my first step on the path to betrayal, the path was ill-defined and as yet had no clear destination. Nonetheless, I wanted to put as much distance as I could between myself and that alien creature with the cool manner and rich robes. And I wanted to calm the anxiety he had inspired in me. So naturally, once I had completed my task, I went for a walk. That is one of life's paradoxes. Though walking is a way into the world, it is also a way of escaping the world. Walking is the resource of the isolated and the solace of the powerless.

* * *

I took the path toward the Two Sisters, since that was the most direct route to the Acequia Nueva, where I hoped to find the Moor. Before reaching the *acequia*, however, the path crossed the way to the plain, a broad mule trail, intermittently cobbled with large untailored stones burnished by countless passing hooves. It was at this junction that I happened to meet the Factor.

As the agent of the proprietary monastery, the Factor would never have been a popular man. I hardly need tell you, my lords, but in the modern world the costs of poverty are considerable, and to maintain the simplicity of a godly life, the religious houses employ men of such ruthless dispositions they make ordinary merchants seem charitable. In fact, it has been my experience that merchants frequently are the more charitable. Uneasy about the fruits of their commerce, they give more generously than men who are more confident of their virtue. But even by the standards of his type, the Factor was unusually scrupulous in extracting every last mite of the monastery's due, plus a supplementary portion on his own account. As a result, the common resentment of his profession was compounded, and his appearance in the community was greeted with as much gladness as the growth of a canker. To make matters worse, he was not favored by the hazards of external form. This was a man who looked like he belonged high on a cathedral wall spouting dirty water from his mouth. Perhaps the knowledge of his own ugliness contributed to his temperament, I do not know, but he seemed always to be looking for a way to exact some retribution from the world, and was used to tax us well beyond the tithe stipulated by his masters.

In my haste to escape the Inquisitor, I did not at first notice the Factor. He was sitting at the edge of an orchard, munching an apple, his mascot lamb curled on his lap, his hobbled mule cropping the grass higher up the hillside. By the time I saw him, it was too late to turn aside. His manner was courteous enough when he hailed me, he even offered me a bite of his apple, but I knew he was a man to be mistrusted, and in his case I had no cause to ignore my parents' warnings. It was thanks to this man that we were regularly reduced to a winter diet of chestnuts. I wanted nothing to do with him.

"Where are you going?" he asked, equably accepting my refusal of his apple and inspecting the uneaten side, as if looking for a weak point by which to attack it.

"Nowhere," I said, truthfully in a sense, for I had no specific destination. I hoped to meet the Moor. I thought I might find him on the Acequia Nueva or by the Two Sisters, but I would as readily have turned aside if it took my fancy to bathe in one of the torrents. I was not going anywhere. The best walks never do. That is the other great adventure of walking. Walking aimlessly, going where you will, you are vulnerable, open to chance, both good and bad, and as such are fully experiencing life. If you set yourself a destination, at least one to which you feel bound to stick rigidly, you are limiting the possibilities. Remember this, you men who are so set on salvation.

"I'll warrant you're off to that stranger you children are so fond of," said the Factor, taking a large bite from the apple, having found its weak point. He ate contentedly for a while, then, when I still did not reply, said: "You may as well go. He won't be here for long."

At that stage, despite the recent interview, I had still not understood the connection between the Inquisitor's visit and the Moor, so I was confused by this statement. Nobody went anywhere from the *aldea*, certainly not the Moor. The Factor toured the region; very occasionally my father had sufficient surplus to descend to the valley; there were the mountains we all roamed according to necessity and inclination; but no one went away. I understood, though, that there was some matter here that might concern me. As the Moor often said, a snake on the path is useful; it makes us alert to what is around us.

When I asked the Factor what he meant by his comments, he looked at me closely for the first time. There was a horrible warmth in his regard.

"He's a witch," he said. "And shall be burned as such."

"He's not!"

"He is," said the Factor, discarding the remains of his apple and turning to pet his lamb. This business of the lamb was a telling perversion in a man otherwise devoid of sentimentality. Ranging as he did across various territories of diverse elevations in which the seasons were retarded or advanced accordingly, the Factor encountered a succession of lambings, and at each term, he would take one of the flock for himself. As a consequence, for a considerable part of the year, he was accompanied by a lamb, which he treated with all the elaborate fondness an indulgent parent bestows on a child. He kept it with him at all times, fed it from a gourd with a leather nipple made specially for the purpose, and would stroke it and murmur to it until it was quite without fear. Then, when it began to mature and the oblique bones of its head made what had been soft and pretty hard and ugly, he would kill it, slitting its throat with his own hands. Once the lamb was eaten, he would move up the mountain to the next birthing, to take another lamb, that would in turn be loved till the time came for its own death.

Holding the lamb in front of his face and gazing into its soft eyes, he repeated his assertion: "He is. He's a witch. He's killed children. He eats babies. Like the Jews do. That's why the Inquisitor is here. To deal with him." Tucking the lamb's head under his chin, he glanced over at me. "Why do you look so worried? Come here, boy. It is of no matter to you. You're a good little Christian, aren't you?"

At the time I did not question why he, claiming the Moor a child murderer, should so calmly say I need not worry. I was too distressed by what he had told me. That people were garroted and burned was not news to me. I had heard tell of these things. But these events were so far distant, they had as little meaning as my parents' memories of their former home. These were matters from another world.

I did not reply to the Factor, or even break step as he called after me, but ran up the mountain, determined to find the Moor and warn him of this terrible threat. I had a destination. Walking where I willed was a thing of the past.

* * *

When I look back at that time now, the Moor and the mountain are indivisible, like motes of dust in the sun. Without the sun's rays, the dust is invisible, but without the dust, the rays of sun are not distinct in the air. So it was with the Moor and the mountain. I cannot see one without the other.

I have been in many mountains since, and higher, too, than those I knew then, but none are so real in the mind's eye as the mountains of my childhood. Anyone wanting evidence for the teleological argument need go no further than the *aldea*. Of itself it was, and probably still is, for things change little and slow up there, nothing better than a cluster of mean hovels, but like the paste jewel between a harlot's breasts (I do all I can, my lords, to make your job easier), it takes splendor from its setting. The hillside immediately above the settlement is

gentle, patched with coppices and latticed with low
stone walls raised as windbreaks to shelter the village *huertas*, and even the higher slopes, mantled by
a great green blanket of chestnut trees, seem shaped
by a familiar hand. But beyond the land patterned
by man, the design is on a grander scale, the open
rock-pocked pasture climbing steeply, sculpted by
a power beyond our poor understanding, cased by
bare cliffs and lozenged with the delicate encaustic
of interlacing watersheds. Sentinel crags stand tall,
like heralds for the high crests to the North, and
all below becomes small and quiet, reduced by
distance to a cunningly woven tapestry, in which
one color leaches into another, and the divisions
of humankind are indistinct. It is on the southern
side of the range, the *solana*, in opposition, I like to
think, to your great city on the *umbría*; and though
my people knew little more than misery and want,
though I long since turned my back on them and
their ways, though I lived there in terror and left
with bitterness, it is a place I recall with wonder and
fondness. In memory, every day is bathed in sunlight, a sunlight that lay on the land as if sedated
by its own heat, bewitched by the contours of the
mountain, hugging the earth heedless of seasonal
humors, holding close the flowers and soft swaying
grass of spring and summer, gilding the shifting

shroud of crisp dead leaves in autumn, and waking countless winking diamonds in the winter snow. And always, in and around that lovely mountain, there is the Moor.

I found him that day along the Acequia Nueva, shoring a wall where a breach had been widened by overflowing water. This was a delicate business because the *acequero* had to balance the demands of irrigation against the requirements of the canal itself. Some among my people, persuaded that they must enjoy a greater ingenuity than any infidel, had sought to improve on the traditional system, lining conduits with grit and clay hard-baked by the sun, determined they would lose less of the precious liquid than leaked from the Moor's loose-banked channels. But before long, the soil crumbled, their conduits collapsed, and the water went to waste, for they did not understand that you need seepage to maintain the roots that hold an *acequia* together. With their neatly sealed canals, they starved the vegetation of life, the foundations dried and died, and everything fell apart. It is a lesson men like yourselves, closeted in your grand palaces, conveyed hither and thither in curtained coaches, and clad in fine clothing, would do well to learn. If you are to maintain your position, you needs must let a little life-giving sustenance seep into the humble underpinnings that support you.

The Moor was startled when I grasped him by the arm, babbling in my childish panic that he must take flight for the Inquisitor was here to burn him, and he looked at me in amazement before starting to laugh. He had a low, throaty laugh that began deep in his chest, like a distant army tramping across the plain, then erupted in a great shout of triumph, as if whatever amused him were yet another wondrous sample of an infinite jest he would never fathom, and of which he would never tire. Eventually, he mastered himself sufficiently to ask why the Inquisitor should burn him.

"Because you're a witch," I said, blurting out the Factor's words before I could shut my mouth—as I say, I never mastered the art of *ship-ship*.

Again, that delighted laugh.

"And you dare to meet with a witch?"

"No. I want to say, you're not a witch. But that's what they say. They say you're a witch and the Inquisitor will burn you."

"Who says I am a witch?" When I explained about my meeting with the Factor, he did not laugh as before, but smiled sadly and tousled my hair. "Then perhaps I am," he said.

"I don't believe it," I said.

"Well chosen words," he said. "Sadly, if others do believe, that is enough. What people call a witch rarely has anything to do with sorcery. It is a matter of belief. And if they believe I am a witch and must burn, then I am made a witch and will burn. It is of little account what you or I say or do. It's like the story of the fox who was seen fleeing in panic. Asked why he was running, he said he had heard that the mules were being forced into service. The other creatures laughed, asking what resemblance he bore to a mule. None, said the fox, but if the envious say I'm a mule and I am caught, who will give them the lie?" The Moor then returned to his work, for the breach was not yet dammed and he had to walk the water down that day as there were gates to be opened by the afternoon. I think, though, it was not mere work that made him turn away. He was not so sanguine as he wished me to believe. Placing a stone in the gap, he sighed, and said: "These *acequia* paths, no matter how hard you work, they always fall apart somewhere."

* * *

Ship-ship. When my parents were asleep, I stole from our home, a wedge of bread, a hunk of lard, and a string of peppers tucked inside my shirtfront.

I confess that in choosing our provisions I had not considered any dietary habits the Moor might have preserved, but that brief escapade was hardly well thought out in any aspect. It was in every sort an impossible plan. Even if the Moor had possessed the necessary monies and some practical point of embarkation, it is unlikely he would have got away. Without those things, escape to North Africa was impossible. And even within a more circumscribed locality, the moment was not well chosen for evading detection. The skies were clear, the moon full, and the shadows we cast nearly as dark as during the day. As for the will to escape, I will let him speak for himself. Suffice to say, he was detained by a different notion of liberty, one I did not properly comprehend till lately, when I was warned of your forthcoming visit.

What moved me to such a desperate measure was not what the Inquisitor or Factor had said, not the Moor's own complacence, or the animosity that was increasingly evident among the adult villagers, but the speed with which the other children had turned against him. I had never been alone in my enthrallment to the Moor and great gangs of us would follow him about the mountains in defiance of our parents; but after the appearance of the Inquisitor, my contemporaries forgot the childish pleasures of walking, talking, telling tales, jesting, and fishing for the moon, and were soon hissing insults at the Moor as he went about his business. He behaved as if nothing had changed, but I knew that if his former acolytes had abandoned him, everything had changed.

He can't have been so easy in mind as he pretended, for when I crept into his tiny cabin, in which there was room for little more than a cot and a cooking fire, and touched him gently on the shoulder, he woke with a start and a stifled cry. Moonlight cut an oblong across the room from the low doorway and, recognizing the intruder, he composed his face, for my benefit I think, as his breath still came short and shallow with the shock of his waking. His breathing quietened when I told him of my plan, perhaps stilled by a moment's wild hope, but then he smiled and said: "So we go for one last walk then?" I say 'but' because in retrospect I see that any hope had faded as fast as it flared and he was merely humoring me.

There is a special pleasure to walking by moonlight and I think that as we crept away from the village, *ship-ship*, I was as happy as I have ever been. I was saving my friend and we were alone on the mountain in the magic of a brightly-lit night. Each step in moonlight seems to be a journey of its own and the soft silvering of the landscape makes every small rise and silhouetted tree an event in itself. Robbed of the hard edges and fine detail of daylight, the landscape breathes with the rhythm of your walking, as if conspiring with your progress to create a private perfection of harmony in which there are no barriers between you and the world, only a collusion of beauty and concord. It is when walking at night that I am most at peace with myself, my world, and the adjustments made between the two.

I was puzzled that the Moor should set a course for the mountains, for it had been my intention that we descend toward the plain to try our chances in a world as different from our own as was conceivable. I had never been to the plain, had no notion of what it meant, nor any suspicion that in later years I would view it so ill when contrasted with the mountains. Nowadays, I regard the lowlands as a fitting habitat for people seeking conformity, a flat home for flat souls, where difference is ironed out by congregation, and any man daring to think for himself is bullied into obedience. But that night, intent on saving the Moor, I imagined the plain was a kind of sea on which we might sail away from danger. The Moor, though, insisted we climb toward the mountain tops.

As we walked between the walls of *huertas*, smallholdings and terraces, he gestured at the red crosses daubed on discrete stones, placed there to celebrate the Christian victory and guard against the sort of maledictions of which he was accused, and every time he pointed to a cross, he emitted a low chuckle. His laughter was not mocking, but rather like the decorated letters of a manuscript, a means of marking the text and enriching its message. The mountain and all that pertained to it was his text, the scroll from which he read and drew his lessons. And that moonlit walk was intended as a kind of exegesis for my particular advantage.

Following much the same route I had when seeking him a few days earlier, we passed the Shepherd's Leap, a terrifying place that would have generated a tale among many less gifted storytellers than the Moor. The cliffs, which in that part of the mountain are generally shallow and easily scaled, become sheer at the Shepherd's Leap and the path, hemmed in by the higher crags, skirts the very edge of the precipice. We were accustomed to walk there and the path was wide enough for two laden mules to pass abreast. Nonetheless, there was a certain horrid fascination to the site, and we children would sometimes tip rocks from the lip and listen to hear how long they took to land. There were places where you could drop a rock and hear nothing at all, not because the valley was so far below but because at the bottom of the cliff there were a number of deep holes, similar to those used by the snow-gatherers on the *umbría* for storing ice, and if you judged it right, the rock would just keep falling, deeper and deeper into the depths of the earth. The thought of that seemingly endless fall was one that appalled me but appealed at the same time. I would like to think my fascination stemmed from some instinctive comparison between the fall of the stone and our own fall, plummeting from grace and falling ever deeper into the earth, becoming ever more human the further we fall, but I fear that in my nonage I scarcely knew the story of Adam and Eve, let alone applied it to my own circumstances.

Walking side by side, we climbed above the head of the Acequia Nueva, where the Moor had walked on water, and came within sight of the great summits separating us from the North. Tracing a long arc below the summits, we made our way to the head of the Giant's Steps, from where one can see the entire Southern valley, the *contraviessa* dividing us from the coast, and, on a clear day, that Africa where I fancied the Moor would be safe. In later days, when reading classical texts, any allusion to the Elysian fields or the like would put me in mind of just such a view, though in truth, the lesson the Moor had come to teach me was no work of paradise, or at best it was a lesson in the compromised paradise we make on earth.

Dawn grazed the skyline with a thin rime of oyster gray light as we stopped for what I supposed was a brief repose and sat to admire the prospect unfurling below us. Stretching away to the distant sea, the valleys were creased in complex folds of verdigris and smudged crape. Speckled about their watercourses were the glimmering lights of fires as clusters of cabins, small farms, hamlets, and villages came to life for the day. The pale powdery glow on the horizon gradually ceded to the gilding of the sun and, as the natural light grew brighter, the location of the settlements became more obscure, like fireflies fading against the flare of a torch, until only a faint haze smeared across a buff colored field betrayed where someone was burning green wood. Even though they were now largely invisible, the Moor pointed to each village, hamlet, and *finca* within sight of our eyrie, and named every one of them as he pointed. When he had finished his litany he asked if I knew the meanings of those names, and I had to admit I did not.

"That is understandable," he said. "They are all Arabic names. The Beekeeper's Cave, The White

Stones, The Arches, The Springs, The Place to the East . . . your people have not renamed them. Some places they know by a Frankish word, a few farms are called after the men who live there, but the villages, the rivers, the mountain itself, they are still known by their Arabic names. Why should this be, do you think?"

Again, ignorance was all I had to offer, but not wishing to disappoint him, I suggested in my childish way that it was because my people were too busy surviving to be naming things and that in time these places would be called by Christian words.

"Perhaps they will," he said. "Perhaps you and your children or your grandchildren will find words for your world. But I think not. Listen. When you name a place you make it your own. For near a dozen generations, my people lived here, learned to live with this landscape and make it their own. That is why I am here. I was chosen because I speak your language. But I was kept here because I know this place and it is mine. Even the soldiers had to admit that. Your people have conquered us with their armies. But they have not yet learned the land, not made it their own. Wanting the certainty of ownership, they have failed to rename what was ours. I will not run from here for the simple reason that this land is my land. Not by deed or might, but by right of knowing it, of having walked it time and again, and understanding its names, moods, and occasional whims. That is one reason I will not run away, though I thank you for the love you have shown me. This is my home. I have to stay, what-ever happens to me as a result. The other reason I will not flee is that all those places I named, all with their Arabic names, they are occupied by Christians and there is little chance I would find the help I need to escape. You saw the walls earlier with their red crosses? It is a poor way of saying I am here and this is mine, like an animal marking its terri-tory. Language is always a better way of holding onto things, for with words we carry the spirit of place in our hearts. But it is, for all that, a sign of who has power here. I do not want to be taken in flight like some beast driven by the hunter's pack. I prefer that any danger be faced like a man. Look at your shadow there. It is long. Just as the shadow of a man is long in the early morning, so the shadow of a man grows long when the sun is setting. Let my shadow be long; that is all I ask."

He would hear no denial of this. Even my tears did not move him, or if they did, it was only enough for him to assure me that, no matter what happened to him, his place upon the mountain was assured, so long as one person remembered that he had been there and that it had meant much to him. Even then I knew that 'one person' was me. And now I know there was a greater truth to his bravado. There is more than one paradise and we gain a variety of eternity here on earth by the impact our actions have on other men. For so long as our memory is held in the hearts of others, be it one solitary soul who remembers us with simple unforced affection, we are not dead to this life. We live in the love of others. You may care to make use of this sentiment, my lords.

The comfort was small, though, as we parted some way from the *aldea*. Slinking back into the hamlet, returning so soon to a life I had been ready to forsake, and prepared for a beating from my parents, I felt as desolate as I had been elated the night before. Daylight is a hard master, especially in high summer when it whitens and flattens every living thing. Come the solstice, a silhouette against the sky in the shape of a man looks unbearably fragile, little more than a leaf in the winds of time. Ever since that night, I have preferred moonlight. I am, if it pleases you, a creature of the night. I say that in defiance, for there is nothing so dark as the workings of the Devil done unashamedly in bright sunlight. In the *aldea*, the Inquisitor was under the old lime tree and he was talking to the other children.

* * *

It is perhaps unfair to attribute the Inquisitor's workings to the Devil. He was a subtle man, not prone to simple concepts of good and evil; indeed it is remarkable he attained the position he did, for I never did hear him deal in the moral absolutes to which your kind are given. But no matter how subtle the workings of one's mind, everyone makes choices that serve the Devil one way or another, and the Inquisitor's particular bargain was expressed in the very political, very pragmatic mission he had undertaken.

Though oftentimes belittled by their elders, the treacherous, truthful words of children are potent enough when harnessed to some adult purpose. The suspicions and accusations of jealous neighbors had to be dissembled by a more innocent, disinterested indictment if they were to be dressed in a livery resembling justice, and in his interviews with my contemporaries, the Inquisitor had found the pretext (I will not call it evidence) he needed for arresting the Moor. The trickster always treads a fine line dividing what is merely diverting from a more sinister duplicity, and it was the Moor's misfortune that the simple deceptions he practiced on us children for the purposes of entertainment could, in a different context, be interpreted as confirmation of a more diabolic gift.

Why the other children were so ready to betray one on whom they had formerly doted is a mystery to me. Perhaps they did not, as I did when my turn came, understand that what they said was a betrayal. Or perhaps they were more sensitive than I to the imperatives of community, knew better the costs of exclusion, and reckoned the price too dear for a little fun and fantasy. I do not know, for I never had the occasion to challenge them. But two days after our moonlight vigil, two days after the Inquisitor had spoken to my fellows, the Moor was arrested and accused of witchcraft. It was held that he consorted with creatures of the night (true, in its way, though not as the Inquisitor claimed), that he had his familiars secreted about the mountain in places only he knew (again, true, but not in the malign sense intended), and that, resenting the reclamation of Christian lands by Christian peoples, he had cast spells on his neighbors and spirited away their children to appease the Devil's need for unformed souls. Out of the green wood of childish tales, the Inquisitor had made a smoke screen to cover the political nature of his mission.

We first heard of these details from the Factor. I do not know how he came by the information, for as we soon found, he was no favorite with the Inquisitor. Nor do I know whether the love of bringing bad news had always been in his nature, or was a deformation of character caused by a profession in which his appearance invariably presaged ill tidings. Certainly, people can acquire a taste for the strangest things. I myself later learned to look forward to my duties in the confessional, for through the rituals of repentance and absolution I discovered a curious affection for the crooked ways of human-being, a kind of fondness for the cracked narrative of living, as if the unceasing spool of sin were a story celebrating the invincible folly of mankind. The Factor was, in any case, a sour man, and he made it his business to spread word of misfortune and hardship, even when he was not their immediate agent. It was not, therefore, very surprising that he should happen to be collecting the summer tithe on the day of the Moor's indictment. Touring the village, ferreting out the harvest, weighing and taking, he related with unseemly glee the Moor's crimes and what abysmal tortures the man would suffer.

He had not, however, reckoned with the Inquisitor, who did not care to have his deeds predetermined by speculation, especially in the very particular circumstances of his present inquiry, in which it was the collective conduct of the *aldea* that was of primary importance.

It was as the Factor was leaving our house that the Inquisitor summoned him from across the plaza, where he was again installed under the lime tree. There was an unusually large number of people at home that day, kept from their fields by the twin imperatives of hiding what they could from the Factor and, more frequently, ensuring that what he took above the allotted amount was as small as could be. As a result, almost the entire village witnessed what ensued.

"I hear you are telling of the forthcoming test of faith." The Inquisitor spoke loudly, louder than he needed had his words been intended for the Factor alone.

"Please, your lordship." The Factor turned his bonnet between his fingers, as if seeking a coin concealed in the seam. And he smiled, a smile that so woefully missed its mark one wished he had never essayed it in the first place. There are people whose features are ill made for pleasantry. They are by no means all ugly. Some of the handsomest people I have met could not carry off a smile without inciting a lively misgiving in the beholder, while many a face deemed by convention to be ugly is perfectly suited for expressing pleasure. But the Factor had the misfortune to be at once ugly and misfitted for smiling, and would have been better advised to stick with his habitual scowl. In truth, he was a poor creature, as humble in the face of authority as he was haughty with those over whom he held some small power, and despite everything that happened, I cannot find it in myself to feel anything but pity for the man. His was a blighted, wasted life that did no one any good, and were it not for Christ's mercy, it would have been as well had he never been born. But if the smile was a mistake, his next words were a gross blunder. "I would," he said, ingratiatingly, "I would that everyone knows what justice is to be done, your lordship."

"You are become an expert of justice?"

Even the Factor, eager as he was to cooperate, could tell the Inquisitor expected no reply. At that moment, the Factor's lamb, which had been cavorting among a brood of hens, scattering them with great good humor, came close to its master's legs, and the stricken man picked it up, as if this were in some way a satisfactory riposte to the Inquisitor's question. The contrast between the Factor and his mascot could scarcely have been more marked, for the one was as full of bile and awkwardness as the other was blithe and unperturbed. The Inquisitor looked at the pair with distaste.

"Or," he continued, "are you perhaps lately appointed by the Holy Spanish Inquisition to inquire into truth and justice in this village?"

Recreating this scene in my mind's eye, I believe the Inquisitor was as vexed with his own role in the affair as he was with the Factor's interference. If memory serves, every time he spoke of justice, he spat the word as if it were the cause of a bad taste in his mouth. He knew he was not there to dispense justice. Or perhaps he was simply insulted that the language of fair dealing be sullied by a man so manifestly unjust as the Factor. I think even your lordships are aware that the men you employ to conduct your business, your so-called familiars, do so with little regard for moral finesse. That is what you pay them for: that you may sustain your precious illusions of purity.

The Inquisitor then shifted tack, for though all had understood his questions were rhetorical, he suddenly demanded why the Factor did not reply.

"Please, your lordship," said the Factor, his language that of a chastened little boy, "I did not think it my place to presume. . . ."

"Yet you would presume to tell these people what I am to do and why I am to do it. What is your purpose here, what role do you serve?"

"Please, your lordship. . . ." Every time he used the phrase, he seemed to shrink a little, and the villagers, standing at their doorways, watched implacably as he was cut down to size, for they knew this was a rare sport, one they had never seen before, would probably never see again, and for which they would pay dear; it was as well to enjoy the spectacle while it lasted. "Please, your lordship, I am the Factor," he said, and he named the monastery for whom he worked, at which point the lamb let out a bleat of distress, not I think by way of commentary on the monastery, which in truth was not unusually venal, but because anxiety made the Factor hold the creature too close. "I am here for the tithe."

"You collect grain, do you?"

"And other produce, your lordship," said the Factor, relieved that they had moved on from the elusive matter of justice to a subject about which he felt more confident. "Olives, your lordship, oil, almonds, chestnuts, figs, plums, pears, a little raw silk, though it's poor stuff they produce here and precious hard to find the way they hide it away to sell on the side, and. . . ."

"You collect grain," repeated the Inquisitor, cutting the Factor short just as he was warming to his subject. "A peck here, a peck there, like that hen." There was an audible titter at that, for there was indeed a scrawny-looking bird, recovered from the shock of the lamb's assault, picking its way across the hard packed dirt, pecking at the odd husk or fallen kernel. The laughter was as much for the image as the serendipity, for now that the likeness had been drawn, everyone realized the Factor's self-important strut was not dissimilar to the speculative, head-bobbing stride of a hen. As if conspiring with the spectacle, the hen clucked and inclined its head to squint at the Factor with a look of glazed misgiving. "May I suggest," concluded the Inquisitor, "that you refrain from speculating on matters that do not concern you, and limit yourself to the task for which you have been deemed fit: a peck here, a peck there."

It was more than a peck that morning, and the households the Factor had not already visited paid the price for his public humiliation. But even in their poverty, I think few of his victims found the penalty too high. The pity of it was that the Factor would later seek to exact a more incisive revenge, one that would encompass the Inquisitor as well as ourselves. The moment he turned his back on the

Inquisitor, the scowl returned and it was darker and nastier than I had ever seen it before.

* * *

I hardly need tell you, my lords, that I have, alongside my more conventional scholastic activities, made a study of the Moor's faith. Whatever you choose to think, I never undertook this study as a path to apostasy, nor as a means of nourishing heretical thought in my own faith. But as two painters may paint the same object from different viewpoints and each profit from the perspective of the other, one man's vision of God may inform and amplify another's. That is what I believe and it is a belief, amongst others, that is likely to cost me dear in the coming days, but it is not one I am prepared to deny. Not, at least, for the present. I cannot answer for the future. I know you put people to trials that are hard and strong, and my flesh has been pampered by my strange career. I may yet make another confession, one far less heartfelt and true than the words you read here.

Curious to note that in forcing words from your victims, you function within a framework of truth that is common among Mohammedans. Theirs is a religion that comes of a nomadic people and for a nomadic people all truth lies in language, for that is the repository of their learning, culture, and identity. You will recall what the Moor said about language and the importance of place names. That was a simple expression of his heritage. In this manner, there are strands of Arabic poetry wherein the form of the verse and the fine phrasing of sentiment are considered more noteworthy than the content and thought. I do not think this emphasis on externals and symbolic representation is always a good thing. Among the Mohammedans and Jews it has, with notable exceptions, lead to religions in which observance of the forms of faith is more important than faith itself. So long as the outward rituals are expressed, the inner conviction is considered sound. In similar but more brutal manner, you, my lords, compel meaningless words from people, careless of heartfelt conviction. Like a dog in a choir stall, you hear the sounds but do not catch the meaning. Nonetheless, language and its impact on belief and conduct can be beneficent, too.

As far as I have been able to determine, Arabic words derive from a verb whose root expresses some basic action. Where we would say 'to be,' Arabic uses a discrete verb, for instance, to say that somebody is beautiful. As a result, their language can sometimes lack the fine gradation of our own more versatile tongues, but it never lacks commitment. It is always there, in the world, and at its heart is the original divine injunction that we should act.

I speak of this because I now see that, in his own, primitive, unlettered way, that was what the Moor was showing us. When he took us tramping across the mountain, we were walking into the world, and in telling his stories, in walking and talking, he was giving us a lesson in being and doing, in engaging with the immediacy of the world around us. Doubtless you, my lords, burdened as you are by a dismal obsession with death, will regard this as the most fantastic nonsense. Nonetheless, I would like to explain something of what the Moor represented to me, of his engagement with the world, the vitality of his being and doing, for it was not something that he surrendered with his liberty. Even in his cell, he was right there, with and in the world, though it may seem that in recounting his imprisonment, I speak of some otherworldly engagement.

He was being kept in his own stone cabin, but I call it a cell, for in truth it had never been much better than that, and with the addition of a bolt on the outside of the door, its modest homely qualities were all but dissipated. I should add that detaining the Moor in his own dwelling was not an act of

kindness. We had no gaol in the *aldea* and his resi-
dence in the meanest of the hovels meant there was
nowhere lower for him to go, 'less it be a byre, but
these were all open on one side and unsuited to
securing a prisoner.

The moon was still large when I went to see
him, but rising late, so that the midnight sky was
nothing but a great black dome flecked with stars.
I remember this clearly, for after he had refused my
offers of food and dismissed my concerns for his
physical well-being (the conversation conducted
though the aperture of his chimney, since the hasp
securing the door was too tight for my childish
fingers), he asked me to describe the sky.

I was at a loss. To describe the sky! I could not
count the stars, had no words to distinguish one
shade of darkness from another, and knew no constellations. But he did not need the description for
himself. He knew it all, carried the skies in his head.
It was simply one more lesson in engaging with the
world. Perhaps it comforted him, too. Directing
my eyes, perhaps he saw these things anew, or
was reminded of how they had looked the first time
he saw them. I hope there was some consolation
there for him.

"Look to the chapel," he said.

"But I can't see it," I said. "Pepe's wall is too high."

"But you know where it is. You can place it in your mind and look in that direction, yes? Now look up, directly above the chapel. What do you see?"

"Night sky."

"And in the sky?"

"Stars."

"And in the stars?"

But I could see nothing.

"Is there not one that is a little larger than the others? And to its left another with a yellow haze about its points?"

Staring at the sky, I saw the stars he meant. And so he began to trace for me the first of the sky's constellations. We continued like that the whole night long, he blinded by the stone walls and wattle roof, but seeing it all, training my own eyes, which were until then unhampered but unseeing, and showing me the shapes of the sky until I began to see them for myself, and was soon describing for him, describing as he had first demanded, the world without, tracing patterns in the sky.

Naturally, I did not identify the constellations accurately, but he recognized my constellations, and would tell me their proper name, all the while assuring me that what I saw in the sky was no less real than what scholars and mariners had identified. Much later, I realized he was teaching me how to see. We all look at the world, even you, my lords, whose eyes are firmly fixed on another kind of heaven, but those who really see it are rare. There are paintings I have known that made me want to weep, for looking at them one knows the artist had a gift for seeing that no amount of training will cultivate. But even lacking that special gift, we can take the time to look and teach ourselves to see something of the world we are in. Seeing, like being and doing, is a part of my testament.

That night I went to comfort the Moor, but comfort flowed in the opposite direction, for it was not merely the gift of seeing he gave me, but a confirmation of God's ubiquity. Looking at the stars, we bear witness to God. Time and again on my travels, driven hither and thither by the demands of high estate in the Holy Roman Church, I have felt myself displaced, lost to the moorings of place and time, just as I have always been a little displaced, ever since my removal from the *aldea*. But I know that in those moments when faith or comfort is weak, when I long to belong or begin to doubt I belong anywhere, I need only look at the night sky, for it is the same wherever we go, and in watching the stars we may anchor ourselves in the world wherever we are.

Moreover, the understanding that my constellations are as valid as the more widely accepted forms
has confirmed in me that trace of Gnostic illumina-
tion of which you are so rightly suspicious. Rightly,
because it undermines your power, for if there is
an interior knowledge of God, you may no longer
cow the people into believing you are the only con-
duit to salvation, and in thinking and believing for
themselves, they will see your authority for the thin
charade that it is.

That night, once we were drunk with describing
the skies, I with my visual senses blurred by looking
(one can only see so much at a time), the Moor with
his mind's eye blunted by countless memories, he
told me a story, which I now know to have been a
debased version of the great novel by Ibn Tufayl.
How he came by this tale, I do not know, for he was
quite without letters and, even had he been able to
read, would in all likelihood, living in that place,
never have seen a manuscript. I can only suppose
that his people maintained an oral tradition of their
faith, much as we rely on pictorial representations
of Christ's life in order to teach faith to our own
illiterate population.

The story recounts how a young boy called
Hayyâ grows up in isolation on an uninhabited
island and investigates life through the power of

innate reason. Observing the world and deducing its nature from his observations, he passes through successive stages of spiritual development, each lasting seven years. Achieving an understanding of the ultimate nature of the universe, Hayyâ, by this time a grown man, goes out into the world and discovers that his understanding is no different from that of the highest authorities representing revealed religion. We will talk more on this later, if you leave me the time, my lords, but for the moment, all I would say is that in Arabic *hayyâ* means 'walk on.' Remember that, my lords, walk on, walk on. The title of the book, in case you are ignorant of this interesting text, is *Hayyâ ibn yaqzhân*. It translates as 'walk on, you bright boy.'

Later, long after the moon had risen, the Moor said I should return to my home, for he did not want me to receive another beating on his account. I had already risked enough by coming to see him. I should get back to my cot. But there was one thing. I had asked if I could bring him something. He had all the food he needed. And it was not an absolutely necessary thing he asked for. But if I could, he would dearly love a skinful of wine.

Walk on, you bright boy, walk on!

* * *

Our Christian poets, even the greatest, tend to regard the most elevated love as spiritual, denying sensuality, but I have always had a weakness for the Mohammedan attachment to the sensual. For them physical beauty is timeless and impersonal. They do not describe an individual, but evoke physical beauty by comparisons with the sun or the moon, sublimating sensuality at the same time as they praise it. When they talk of wine, though, there is no such ambiguity. In their Bacchic poems, the sensual delight of drunkenness is a metaphor for spiritual ecstasy. Wine, my lords, is a way of knowing God.

Were you willing to discuss the matter, you might claim we Christians know God through communion, but there is a world of difference between celebrating the divine by getting drunk oneself and watching someone else sip the blood of Christ on one's behalf. Again, we need no proxy between us and God, and a symbolic act of anthropophagi cannot be compared to a personal encounter with divine drunkenness. Hark you well, my lords, for the theft of this gift is one I have never yet confessed and may be of some help to you in discrediting my character.

It must have been a moment of weakness on the Moor's part, for he would never normally have placed me in danger, yet he knew full well there was no wine to be had in the *aldea*. My milk and cider people had yet to learn the pleasures of the vine and the only wine we saw had either been made by the Moor from the grapes grown on the small patch of land he was allowed to cultivate for himself, or had been raised high in a chalice before an altar in one of the large towns toward the plain. The only Christian man among our company to have acquired a taste for wine was the Factor, who sought to ape his masters and had learned to drink wine with his meals. I know not where he got his supplies, but I fancy they must have come from the *solana* of the *contraviessa*, where the vines planted by the Moors for commercial purposes still flourished.

When not compelled by matters of business, the Factor did not reside among us, but maintained a house in the valley. For short visits, though, he had a cave an hour's easy walking from the *aldea*. You may misdoubt this, you who have known nothing but palaces and sheltering cloisters. For you, any troglodyte who is not a professed anchorite is little better than a heathen, possibly less than that, for he is without society and has no faith at all, but in the mountains, many men live in caves and some live well. It is true, most of the caves around the *aldea* were unfit for human habitation, being little more than shallow overhangs, suited only for corralling animals, but there were one or two that were large, dry, and salubrious. Warm in winter and cool in summer, these caves were greatly valued among the people of the mountain, and the Factor's was among the finest.

Many wondered why he kept a cave, for though it was known to be a good cave and was rumored to house somewhere in its depths a treasure hidden by a departing Moorish prince, it was hard of access and infrequently used by the man who had claimed it for his own. Later I understood why he wanted such a cave; but at the time, if indeed I ever thought about it, I would have said he kept it as he kept everything, in order to have something other people desired and might have used more profitably than him.

I have spoken earlier of the Shepherd's Leap and the snow-holes at the base of the cliff. To reach the Factor's cave, one had to follow the stream below the cliffs, skirting the holes and winding between the base of the cliffs and the bed of the stream, until one reached an impasse, just to the left of which was the entrance to the cave. There was a quicker way, following the Acequia Nueva above the cliffs, then descending the rock face further up; but this approach was risky, for though less sheer than the Shepherd's Leap, the cliffs were still precipitous and not to be chanced without some compelling motive. The afternoon following my interview with the Moor, I made my way along the stream, clutching a gourd taken from home and the wineskin the Moor had squeezed under his ill-fitting door.

I knew the Factor was absent and not due back for another three days, but even so, as I approached his cave I was subject to a horrible dread. This was not a man one crossed. We were taught to avoid him and told that, if we did have the misfortune to meet him, we should do all we could to avoid upsetting him. Breaking into his cave in order to steal wine was an act of folly that might cost me and my family dear. But, emboldened by my friend's predicament, I approached the façade of the cave.

A wall had been built across the entrance and the door was secured with a rudimentary lock, but a gap had been left at the top left-hand corner of the wall to let smoke escape. The mortar between the stones was old and crumbling, exposing many handholds, and I had no difficulty clambering up to the opening, from where I could peer into the cave. It was dark inside, but I could just make out the shape of a cot and a rude table, and see below me a shallow stone trough filled with the charcoal of the Factor's last fire. That was all. It was hardly comforting to know that the greater part of the cave was invisible from my vantage point, that anyone or any *thing* might be waiting in there, but a peculiar kind of pride propelled me forward, and I slithered through the aperture, dropping onto the cold coals. There was a sharp cracking as I landed and a cloud of dust arose, causing me to choke and cough, noises that echoed unpleasantly in the confined space.

When I had recovered my breath, I waited awhile, listening, half imagining I heard a soft breathing from the depths of the cave. Dismissing the notion as a fancy conjured by fear, I ventured toward the table, hoping to see something more from there. The wood was rough and deeply scored about the edges where some sharp instrument had been used repeatedly, presumably to cut bread or meat, but there was not enough light to see beyond the table and I daren't start a fire, lest the smoke attract attention. There was also a curious smell of corruption, not strong, but unpleasantly sweet and intrusively rank at the same time, akin to the cadaver of a goat discarded in a secluded corner of the mountain and left to bloat.

Gradually, my eyes grew accustomed to the dark, but with only the light from the smoke-hole it was still so obscure I realized I would have to conduct my search by touch rather than sight. It was not a pleasant thought. Feeling my way through the lair of such a loathsome being, I was persuaded I would sooner or later touch something horrible, maybe even the patiently waiting man himself; but even as a child, once embarked on a course of action, it was not in my nature to stop till the task had been achieved. I felt my way round the table, then stretched out my arms and moved away from both cot and table, groping for the wall, reasoning that the wine, if wine there was, would be stored near the table.

The wall was dry and rough and left a fine powder on my fingers, as if it had been washed with lime, though, given the gloom, this was clearly impossible. Doubtless some mineral deposit covered the rock, for where a cave had once been damp and later dried, you would often find such grainy matter coating the walls. Glancing back, I was reassured to see the beam of light slanting down from the smoke vent. The light was more clearly defined from this perspective and I felt that, no matter how deep I went, I would be able to find my way back to the exit. Feeling my way along the wall, I encountered a chest full of cloths and some shelves laden with clay jars, but in none of them was there anything resembling wine.

Beyond the shelves, the floor of the cave sloped very slightly but perceptibly in my heightened state of awareness, and I sensed rather than felt the walls narrowing. Keeping one hand on the wall I had been following, I stretched out the other to feel for the opposing wall. And so I progressed, like a novice tumbler, precariously balanced between the wall I touched and the wall I sought, edging my feet forward, using them as feelers for any obstacle. It is a common enough means of progress in life, my lords, keeping one hand on the familiar while groping for its counterpart.

At one point, my hand brushed against something hanging from the roof, something long and soft like fine goat's hair, and I recoiled with exaggerated disgust, till I realized it must have been a clump of cobweb. Looking back to the light from the entrance, I confirmed this hypothesis. I was already deep into the cave, maybe forty adult paces. It would be entirely in order if the Factor, who was as perfunctory as anyone in the *aldea* when it came to matters of cleanliness, had not troubled himself with cobwebs this far from his living quarters.

Logically, I ought then to have turned back. Wine would not be stored in this chthonian corner. It would be near the entrance and the table, where it was required. But somehow, the search for the opposing wall had become compelling in itself, and I decided to continue just a little further.

As I progressed deeper into the cave, the smell grew more intense, and I began to regret not turning back earlier; but having begun the search, I desperately wanted to find that opposing wall, as if in some way my quest for wine, for which in truth I no longer gave a fig, would be incomplete until I touched the cave's opposing side, and I would in consequence be dogged by a sense of having failed to do my best.

Then my foot, having carefully sought opposition and finding none, met not with the solid stone of the cave floor, but something round and mobile that rolled, nearly overturning me in the process, and setting off a dry, brittle clatter. When I had recovered from my shock, I realized that this had to be a pile of wood I had stumbled over. Doubtless the Factor kept a store at the back of the cave to ensure he always had dry wood. I might have bent and touched the object to confirm this, but I did not, for at that moment . . . well. . . .

Let me say here that I will never know if what I am about to tell you is true. For reasons that will become clear, I hope and pray to God that it is not, for the implications are too horrible to contemplate.

Time may heal, my lords, but always at the cost of decay.

As I considered bending to touch whatever I had trodden on, unwilling to do so, but wanting nonetheless to know (the desire for knowledge has always been a weakness of mine, my lords), at that moment, I heard, or thought I heard, something groan in the very depths of the cave. I still cannot swear I heard this sound, that it was not a gust of wind given voice by the vaulting, or the grating of a rock dislodged by my recent stumble, but at the time I believed I had heard it. Belief was enough to tip my suppressed dread into outright panic.

Terrified, I turned and fled, desperate to escape whatever it was that was stirring in the recesses of the cave. I staggered over loose stones, tripped on a stool, scrambling pell-mell for the circle of light that would save me, eventually colliding with the table and bouncing off toward the far wall, where I fell on some wooden object and grazed my head on the rock.

I believe I lost consciousness for a moment. The next thing I knew, I was looking at my hand, marveling at how thin my blood was and trying to understand why I was bleeding from beyond the reach of my arm, as if my blood were all around me and seeping back toward my body rather than

draining away from it. Then I saw that the wooden
object over which I had fallen was a small barrel,
and leaking from its rough wooden spigot were
gouts of black wine.

As it transpired, the simple outlines of percep-
tion had been colored by fancy, for when at length
I found myself in the open air and sufficiently far
from the horrible cave to pause and examine the
liquid I had hastily tipped into my receptacles, I discovered it was not the blood dark wine I had imagined, but a cloudy brown liquid, similar to the *costa*
that is now common in that region. Moved by curi-
osity and an urge to still my beating heart, I tasted
the wine, which proved sweet and appealed to my
childish palate. After the first few tentative sips, I
became greedy for this newfound nectar, and began
gulping, as if such dulcet ambrosia might dispel
the horrible fancies fear had conjured in the cave. I
might not have wanted a bite of the Factor's apple,
but I was ready to drink his wine. Before long, the
gourd was empty. Having taken such appalling
risks for his sake, I could not return to the Moor
empty-handed, so I resisted the temptation to start
on the wineskin and endeavored to get to my feet.

Needless to say, in this, my first experiment
with Bacchus, I was like every neophyte, a lurching
elated fool. I will not detail my erratic progress back

to the *aldea*. Suffice to say, I fell in the river twice, crawled round the snow-holes like a baby, and reeled into a tree that had unaccountably leaped out of the woods to straddle the path. In one's first encounter with divinity, one is inevitably tongue-tied, for the language is new and the effects of trying to master its intricacies are mystifying. But even then, I knew this was an idiom I would enjoy.

Having spoken the language of wine many times since, I often wonder at the Mohammedans' rejection of this gift from God. If my understanding is correct, they have turned away from that great tradition they cultivated on the Peninsula and, formerly, I believe, elsewhere. They claim their Koran forbids the fermenting of the earth's fruits, that it is ungodly to drink, and that sobriety is a condition of salvation. This is strange, is it not, for the same book also claims paradise is gained by making one's companions laugh, that jesting is a just way to enter heaven's gates. Can it be that they, too, like you, my lords, in your own way, have found the light of God's grace too bright? Is this the weakness of all revealed religion, that faced with the numinous it has to hedge God in with the dark ledgers of regulation? Is sobriety really a condition of salvation? Is condemnation the key to heaven?

Drink wine, my lords, drink and laugh, be done with your shadowy search for a difference you deem culpable. God did not intend us for cold sobriety, nor the rigid observation of ritual. Put aside your narrowing notions of what is right; drink, laugh, and love the life you have been given. Only then will you please God.

I do not recall how I contrived to conceal my drunkenness from my parents. I suppose the simple fact was so improbable it never occurred to them that I might have been drinking wine, while the cuts and grazes from my fall were explanation enough of my malaise. Despite the pounding in my head (no matter how enlightening, an encounter with God is always a little bruising), I forced myself from my cot that night and crept to the Moor's cell, and dropped his wineskin through the chimney. He blessed me for my initiative.

Walk on, bright boy, walk on!

* * *

Take a turn round the mountain *pueblos* of the South and you will see that every farm has planted behind it a hedge of Barbary figs. This plant is most benef-icent, for it possesses a remarkable capacity for absorbing ordure, turning the most noxious fecal matter into a nourishing sweet fruit. I am compelled to say that there are people of my acquaintance whom I can only conclude are nature's counter-weight to the Barbary fig for all the good they do the world, serving no higher purpose than turning perfectly good food into fecal matter. You see, my lords, I am not wholly free from the darker side of Gnosticism. Such sentiments are hardly moved by Christian charity, yet this is a reflection to which I have had recourse time and again during my career in the church. The first time I felt it, the first time I knew this bitter demon that resides within me (for it is both bitter and demonic), was on the day of the Moor's trial.

I do not say that everyone who participated in those events was worthless nor lacking in any merit that earned them the gift of life. However, at the time, I was so appalled that people could turn away from one who had been their neighbor, could denounce him with what seemed such scant com-punction, that I promised myself, if ever I got away from that place, I would never return, nor show any sign of life to those who had been my kith and kin. It is a promise which, with one notable exception, I have kept.

The trial was conducted in the plaza and was open to all who cared to attend, the villagers lined around the square, the Inquisitor in his usual place under the lime tree, and the accused tied to a door post at some distance from his principal accusers. This public proceeding was a rarity and had attracted many people from surrounding communities, as had been intended. They believed they were there for the entertainment, but I now realize their presence was required for the fulfillment of the Inquisitor's political purpose. And, of course, there was the necessity of making my own betrayal public.

I will not bore you with details. You, my lords, know only too well how these things may be staged. The charges were read aloud, in Latin for the most part, the better to impress the people with the gravity of the crimes, but with specific charges of infanticide and witchcraft made clear in the vernacular, eliciting gasps of horror from the crowd and causing the woman whose grief had given rise to the first accusations to weep loudly. Then the witnesses were brought forward to rehearse their testimony, telling of the Moor's peculiarities, of suspicious habits, eccentricities, his unnatural influence on the children of that place, and of his isolation from the rest of the community. This last charge was most disgraceful, as the Moor had never been anything but accommodating, despite his circumstances, and if he was isolated from the rest of the community, it was the work of everyone else, not of the Moor.

I was surprised that so many people were called to testify, my own parents included, for though their resentments and grievances were common, the reiteration of so many minor suspicions, few varying in their material, none in tenor, seemed scarcely germane to the matter. Moreover, as I now know, your organization does not favor public accusation, but prefers anonymous denunciation followed by public repentance. It is always the way of those who proclaim light yet live in darkness. But the Inquisitor was not seeking precision or relevance, nor did he require repentance. For his purposes, numbers were more important than pertinence, and it was essential that those who bore witness did so in public, that each may know his neighbor's complicity in the affair. Even the children, whom I had seen talking to the Inquisitor but a few days before, were called upon to repeat how the Moor knew 'secrets,' how he could create illusions, how he made them see things that were not real . . . but of that the best was kept for me.

When my name was called, I thought the clerk, a familiar brought there by the Inquisitor for the proceedings, had made a mistake. I had given no testimony, understood nothing of these charges but that they were false, was not one of those who had gone hurrying to authority with accusations, suspicions, or grievances, imagined or otherwise. Yet the clerk repeated my name and my parents urged me forward.

As I stepped into the center of the plaza and approached the lime tree, I glanced at the Moor. Tethered as he was like a beast to a post, there was little he could do to encourage me, save smile and indicate with a nod of the head that I should do as I was bid. And I believe he may have murmured something. His lips seemed to move, ever so slightly, too slightly to really articulate, but I fancy he whispered *ship-ship*.

"You were the accused's special friend?" inquired the Inquisitor after the preliminaries were done.

"I am his friend," I said, and the audience exclaimed again, this time with a different kind of shock.

In those two sentences was the nub of the matter, for it was as the Moor's 'special friend' that my testimony was needed, and it was by declaring the continuation of that friendship that I began my voyage from the village, though there were other, more practical reasons than my own safety that motivated my removal. I am, in any case, glad that my betrayal, when it came, was not a willing betrayal, that I did not deny my friend, even if I subsequently inculpated him.

"You have heard what the other children of this place have said about this man. Of how he enchanted them and played tricks, initiated them into secrets. Do you have anything to add to what they said?"

I said nothing, not knowing what to say, for the words the other children had spoken had not been untrue, but had been used to imply an untruth. Nothing they had described had not happened. But it had all been in fun, there had been nothing sinister about it. And yet, if I confirmed what they said, I would be adding my voice to the accusations. So I held my tongue.

"You do not deny that the things they described happened?" persisted the Inquisitor.

Again the silence, interrupted only by my father hissing my name, for he knew the obloquy that would fall upon us all if his child was the only one not to denounce the Moor. At length, unable to answer the question without harming the Moor, I said, as I had during our previous encounter: "The Moor is a good man."

"That is for this inquiry to decide," said the Inquisitor, hastily, doubtless unwilling to have questions of good and evil brought into play. He was, as

I say, not of your ilk, my lords, and knew that the less said about morality, the easier his task would be. "Can you tell me what you did with the accused when you went together on the mountain?"

Here I felt I was on safer ground.

"We walked," I said.

Surely, nobody could find fault in walking?

"You walked? And where did you walk?"

"Everywhere. Nowhere special. Just the mountain."

"Then to what purpose did you walk?"

The question of purpose, like the earlier matter of 'manners' in men and stories, was new to me, but after that moonlit night striding across the mountains, I had begun to see that the walking was important, and that if the Moor were taken away from me, I would have to keep walking to conjure him again. I was not, therefore, wholly unprepared for the question.

"For pleasure," I said.

At that my people laughed, for the idea that one might walk for pleasure was as strange to them as a pig with two heads: they had heard of such freaks, maybe knew someone who claimed to have seen a comparable phenomenon, but could in no wise imagine it as a tangible truth. One walked to sow and reap, one walked to hunt and herd, one walked because one was too poor to do otherwise, but one did not walk for pleasure.

"For pleasure? What pleasure did you take from walking? Did the walks lead to some reward? Were you recompensed for your labors? Were they comical in some way?"

It seemed the Inquisitor was as bemused as my people were, but he was not a man readily bemused. His talk was tendentious and, though no one else had spoken openly of it, he knew precisely where we were going.

"It was all of those things," I said, "and none at the same time." That Jesuitical response did take him aback and may have been the moment when he first glimpsed my future. "Walking is its own reward. You don't do it to get anything." Again my people tittered, but less certainly this time, more uneasily, for they sensed I was not playing the fool, but describing something they themselves did not know. "You do it for itself," I continued, encouraged by the queer experience of thinking for myself, momentarily forgetting the Moor's plight. "For moving your body and being on the mountain. You feel freer. As if walking, you can go anywhere, do anything you want."

That, incidentally, is a credo to which I still hold.

"And the comical aspect? Did the mountain make you laugh? Did *he* make you laugh?"

I might have given him away then, because I had indeed laughed. All the children had. Laughed and remembered. It must have been their memories that alerted the Inquisitor to this trick and its potential as evidence of the Moor's sorcery. Instead, though, I said: "The mountains can make you laugh. That valley there looks like my mother when my father lies on her."

I still do not know how I had the temerity to say this. Ours was a small house and, like most children my age, I had seen replicated in haste and darkness the couplings animals conducted without shame in broad daylight. Even so, we knew better than to talk of such things. Yet the mirroring of form was something I had noted several times. The valley directly behind the *aldea* was framed by two small hills that, with the flanks of the valley tapering to a crux at its head, perfectly matched the knees of a recumbent woman with her legs raised and parted. Think on it, my lords, if ever you go to the mountain. It may do you some good.

My mother shrieked, the Moor unwisely let out a bark of laughter, several of our neighbors were hard put to stifle their own amusement, and even the Inquisitor, whom I never knew to crack a smile, seemed briefly to bite his lower lip.

Gradually the hubbub settled and my father calmed my mother. The fault was not forgotten, though. The beating I received that night was severe, the more so since my mother's embarrassment was fortified by my father's anger at my attempted defense of the Moor.

The Inquisitor tried again: "I had in mind," he said, "some spectacle inherent in the walking itself rather than any picture imagined in the landscape. Did you run, hop, turn somersaults, walk on your hands, anything of that nature?"

Emboldened by the success of my previous sally, I wracked my brains for some spectacle that came from our own movements. The Moor's plight was almost entirely forgotten. I had never spoken publicly before and found after the initial unease that it was a pleasure to talk and have so many people listen. But I could think of no such antics to please the Inquisitor.

"Perhaps he walked in the sky," suggested some wit from the back of the crowd. Whether he had been primed in this or was simply inspired by the account of fishing for the moon that had been told earlier in the proceedings, I do not know, but it helped nudge us along.

Outraged by the snorts the man's comments elic-
ited, snorts that were half derisive, half fearful, for
my people thought a witch would indeed be able
to walk in the sky, I said: "Why not? He walked on
the water."

To me the one seemed no less remarkable than
the other. The Moor had told us the tale of a boy
with a magic carpet that flew through the air, so
that he might indeed be said to have walked in the
sky. And he himself had walked on water. It was up
at the head of the Acequia Nueva. There had been a
whole group of us there and the Moor had made us
stand well back, saying his magic wouldn't work if
we were too close. We had watched in wonder as he
had walked, albeit precariously, arms outstretched,
on the water running along the center of the *acequia*.
We were near enough to see he wasn't standing on
the wall and there was no ice. He had walked on
water! And when I said that simple sentence, I had
unfortunately flung out my arm in the direction of
the Moor, so there was no denying who had walked
on water.

At first, I did not understand the consternation
this had caused. It was a fine trick, I thought, and
I had successfully answered those sneering critics
who would not believe in miracles. But then I
saw the Inquisitor's face, saw that something had

been accomplished, and heard the hisses around the plaza, bitter whispered words like 'blasphemy' and 'witch.' That, of course, was the only other story I knew of such miraculous walking, Jesus walking on the water to calm his frightened disciples. Jesus walked on water. Moors did not. Or if they did, it was proof positive of some occult and sinister design.

The Inquisitor dismissed me. I looked at the surrounding faces. They were all turned on the Moor. There was no trace of pity. They all looked vindictive. But the Moor was perfectly composed. He simply smiled at me, just as he had when I first took center stage, and shrugged, as if to say this was the way of the world and we were helpless to resist.

Ship-ship.

* * *

No one loses his way on a straight road. Had I not taken part in that fateful trial, my life would not have been shadowed by the memory of betrayal, nor would I have come to my present pass. Yet the straight roads are rare and those who follow them usually find they have made a road that traverses an empty landscape and leads nowhere. Nothing natural and wholesome is entirely straight, and every path to God follows its own warped way. I did not know that then and wanted to put everything right, to reclaim a clear, direct trail unencumbered by hidden motives, half-understood guilt, and obscure shades of meaning. Thus it was that, when the inquiry was done and the crowd dispersed, I chased after the Inquisitor as he strode away to his lodgings, and grasped the hem of his light summer cloak. He turned abruptly and the clerk, seeing the source of this impertinence, made to strike me. I did not flinch, though, and the Inquisitor stayed his underling's hand.

"This is wrong," I said. "The Moor never did these things. Not like you're saying."

Again the clerk moved to rid his master of my irksome importunity, but the Inquisitor stopped him and looked on me for a long while, and again there was that infinitely slight suggestion of humor, a suspicion that he was compelled to lightly bite his lower lip. Doubtless the picture was comical enough. The ragged peasant child, eyes ablaze with indignation, presuming to correct a protector of the true faith. Another man might have been incensed, but the Inquisitor dismissed his clerk and asked me what was wrong.

I cannot recall the precise words of my reply, only that it was long, incoherent, and tearful. It was, however, in sum a repetition of everything I have told here concerning the Moor. That this was a good man given to trickery not to deceive but to instruct and entertain, that he dissimulated life to enhance it, that the specific act of walking on water was not a mockery of Jesus nor bad magic, but a jest designed to amuse. . . .

Despite my disjointed speech, something of what I said, or the manner (that word again) in which I said it, or the sheer force of my indignation must have touched the Inquisitor, for he let my discourse run, and only when I had stuttered to an end did he speak.

"Where exactly were you when the Moor walked on water?" he said.

I did not follow his reasoning; nevertheless, hoping it would in some way help the Moor, I described the place beyond the Shepherd's Leap toward the head of the Acequia Nueva, and offered to take him there myself if he wished. But if I thought mere location might lead to exculpation, I was mistaken.

"That will not be required," he said. "If necessary, I can find the place myself. Indeed, I believe I have seen it before. Your description corresponds with what the others said."

It was a moment before the implications of this statement struck me, but when they did, my dismay at what was happening intensified.

"You knew!"

At first he did not follow me, but when I repeated the accusation, he understood what I meant, and a new respect entered his eyes.

"Yes," he said. "I had heard the story before."

"Then why did I have to tell it? Why did you make me say the Moor walked on water? Any of the children could have said what they told you before."

"What difference would that have made?" he asked. "It would change nothing for the Moor."

"It would have made a difference to me," I said, aware for the first time that my grief was as much for myself as the Moor.

He hesitated for a moment, then clearly took a decision to risk some confidence in me: "The others had already spoken. It was necessary that you speak, too, that the story of walking on water should come from your lips."

I remember noticing he kept using the word necessary. Evidently, the necessities were what had motivated the day's proceedings.

"But you made me say words you knew would hurt him. You made me betray him."

I was infuriated and, had I not thought further conversation might lead to more information or in some way serve the Moor's cause, I think I would have attacked the Inquisitor there and then. My puny fists would have done him no harm, but I have never believed frailty is sufficient excuse for pusillanimity, and have often times engaged in battles I knew I could not win and which would obviously do me no good—have I not, my lords?

"It was necessary that everyone speak." Again, necessity; and again, the Inquisitor seemed hesitant, almost at a loss for words. "There is something St. Paul said, which I will translate for you. He said that in passing judgment on another, man condemns himself, because in judging another, one does the same as that man."

(You may wish to read this for yourselves, my lords. Romans II,i)

"You are the judge," I said. "So you are the same as the Moor."

He looked at me closely. There was a sharp light in his eye, not unfriendly, but irritated and interested at the same time. Perhaps he had already detected affinities I would only identify with the passage of time.

"That is as may be," he said. "But in this case it was necessary that everyone bear witness and everyone be the judge. That is why I deceived you into speaking your piece about walking on water."

"But why? It wasn't fair. Now it's my fault if you. . . ."

I could not at that time say the sentence.

"No, it wasn't fair. But the fault . . . Listen. It is not your fault. Or not your fault alone. It was and is the fault of everyone. Everyone spoke. Everyone shares responsibility. That is what's important. Remember that. It was necessary that everyone participate."

"You don't care if the Moor is innocent?" I demanded.

"His innocence or guilt is not important!" exclaimed the Inquisitor, at last exasperated by my persistence, though he rapidly controlled himself. "Besides, everyone is guilty in their way and a reminder of that guilt is never redundant."

At the time, I did not understand this, but I remembered it afterwards, and now take it for a sign of the Inquisitor's subtlety. I do not think, my lords, he was speaking your language. He was not a man to declare someone guilty, and then set about proving that guilt with the implements of torture. Given time and sufficient cruelty, anyone can be made guilty by those methods. Nor was he talking of his own share of guilt, though I believe he genuinely regretted the falsehoods he propagated to promote unity. Rather, he was speaking of the quotidian guilt that is so necessary (I choose my words carefully, my lords) to humankind. None of us ever do enough to ease the suffering of others. We, who live well and easy, learn to close our ears to the cries of the poor and diseased. We smother public compassion with private comfort and lament injustice without endeavoring to remedy its causes. These are choices we are free to make. Guilt, conscience pricked once in the while, is the dye that distinguishes choice from chance. Nothing is predestined, my lords, nothing.

"But that is not the issue," continued the Inquisitor. "Not now, not here. Listen, you cannot understand this at your age, but maybe later it will mean something to you. It may help you to adapt to the necessary compromises of life. You must understand, we have fought five hundred years to regain this land. Our hold on it is still weak. I do not mean militarily, even emotionally, for we never let it go, not in all those centuries. Indeed, the struggle to regain it was what held us together. But now that we have the land, fighting for it no longer holds us together. Especially here in the South. The people of your village come from a cold climate. Their resolve is softened by the unwonted heat of this place. They have not lived here generation after generation. They need something to hold them together. And if that something is an outsider who commits a crime against their communality, I must deliver them that. The fault, the common testimony, the judgment, and the guilt, if you like . . . these are what will hold your people together and stop them turning against one another."

Of course, I do not remember this speech word for word. The Jesuits admired my memory more than anything else, but I cannot recall every word of what was said seven decades ago. What I do remember, though, are the arguments, for they were repeated many years later when the Inquisitor and I met again, when the curse his protection entailed was made evident. At the time, though, I was struck by the parallels with what the Moor had said that moonlit night about my people being uneasy in the terrain.

"For you, though," he concluded, "I fear that bond is already broken. For you, we will have to find some other solution."

And he turned and walked away, leaving me bewildered, feeling every bit the child, yet immeasurably old, drained of both indignation and understanding, knowing only that this was an unjust

world and that in some obscure way I was partici-
pating in my first lesson in injustice, and that it was,
in the eyes of the world, 'necessary.'

* * *

I was saved the sight of the Moor's execution, not
by any quirk of charity or solicitude, but by intent
to murder.

Though it scarcely seemed so at the time, the
instruction that the Moor be garroted then burned
was a mercy, a mercy for which I was later grateful
to the Inquisitor, who had no cause but pity, or perhaps guilt, to move him to such a breach of prece-
dent. I have seen people burned. The torment they
suffer is terrible, the cruelty compounded by its
futility. For it serves no purpose but to protect the
self-serving piety of a church that would have no
blood on its hands. If the executioner knows his job,
garroting is quicker and altogether less cruel. That
is why it is preserved for those who make public
repentance.

Whether the Moor's executioner knew his job, I
cannot say, for as I stated above, I was not present
when the deed was done. What I can say is that the
result of the inquiry had always been a foregone
conclusion, since the executioner arrived the day

after the business of testimony was over. There was no state executioner within two days ride of the *aldea*. The man had been summoned before the trial took place.

Perhaps that will not trouble you, my lords, but I hope that, in the unlikely event of this manuscript surviving and being read in future centuries, later generations will have learned enough hypocrisy to be shocked by such injustice. I say hypocrisy, my lords, for there is in truth nothing surprising about unfairness, brutality, or baseness in human behavior. If you were to prepare a gazette of any day in history, it would be a catalogue of atrocity. But if we are not to be duped by the extreme dualism that characterizes the Gnosticism of which you accuse me, we must pretend these things are exceptional, we must veil our narratives in hypocrisy. Do not misunderstand me, my lords. I do not seek to excuse myself in your eyes—certainly not in your eyes. I share the Gnostic's faith in inner revelation. What I decry is his lamentable desire to ascribe all matter to a demiurge and declare everything that is of this world to be evil. Pelagius knew better when he stressed the good in human nature. The story of the world is a story of evil, but the good is interwoven with the bad and, if human-being is to be tolerable, a little seemly hypocrisy, a measure of self-deception, is necessary—provided it is leavened by that conscience of which I spoke previously.

Though little willing, I have since witnessed for myself the sad sick sumptuous pageant of an urban auto-da-fé, with royalty in attendance, a grand procession preceding the test, the celebration of mass, the swearing of oaths of obedience, the formal reading of sentence and, at end, what no accumulation of rites can dissimulate, the base business of authorized murder. What took place in the *aldea* was nothing like as ostentatious. But then, as you will have divined, what took place in the *aldea* was a little unusual in every respect, despite the fact that it mirrored similar coups across the country. The Inquisitor, for instance, had been invested with civil as well as spiritual authority, hence the sentence of death, which would not normally have been declared by him—you know of this, my lords, for you are practiced in passing those you condemn to the state, calling them the 'relaxed,' on the understanding that the state will do your dirty work for you, just as you do another kind of dirty work for it. As for the abridged ritual, we were a poor, backward people and, though every hamlet had its role to play in claiming the land, it scarcely needed an imposing ceremony to impress upon us the solemn responsibility we shared. We were a people for whom clubbing to death a cornered rat was a major excitement. Killing a man needed little fanfare. It was its own advertisement.

The *aldea* was crowded, those who had attended the inquiry multiplied tenfold by the inhabitants of a dozen settlements within a day's walk, so that the Moor's death would in some measure serve several communities. Its impact would be less on those who had not testified, but they would still take away with them the image of a man unlike them, a face that would fit the unifying threat they required.

I was in a daze, disbelieving what was about to happen, yet knowing that this exceptional crowd presaged an exceptional event of exceptional injustice. Only four of us, though, would know the full degree of that injustice. Unwilling to remain among the eager mob, I gradually edged away from the plaza, soon leaving the *aldea* altogether, slinking through the fields to avoid the steady stream of people still arriving from the valley trail.

It was an isolation that came easy, for in the short time that had elapsed since the end of the inquiry, I had learned there was no place for me among the people I had called my own. Quite apart from the beating from my father, I had been shunned by my former playmates, even spat upon by one or two older boys, and when an unseen hand had pushed me in the small of the back, causing me to fall, those adults who had witnessed the attack simply turned aside, as if I did not exist. Whatever the Inquisitor said about shared responsibility, it was clear the coming days in the *aldea* would not go well with me.

Fate is a cruel jester, taking paradox for wit and playing mean sport with the emotions of men. Nobody else showed any sign of guilt, but I felt it, felt it with every fiber of my being. I do not mean the healthy guilt of an uneasy conscience, but the dull burden of one who, albeit unwittingly, has betrayed a friend. You, my lords, will not understand the nature of this fidelity, so it is scarcely worth talking of here, for the more I speak, the more my amanuensis writes, the more I suspect this document will never see the light of day, but will be burned after the most cursory glance. But if you do read this far, my lords, I would ask that you think on this. Friendship, loving-kindness, devotion these are among the finest things we may experience. When they are invested in another individual, then betrayed, we betray all humanity, because we deny what is finest about our kind. This is another thing the Gnostics got wrong. Judas is not to be celebrated for performing a *necessary* function in bringing Jesus back to the Godhead. He is to be pitied. For he is the exemplar of all betrayal and consequently of all denial of life and needs must have been the most miserable of men.

My mind was not sufficiently formed to articulate this at the time, but the onus of such thoughts was there, and I gladly distanced myself from my fellows, drifting away from the center of activity toward the mountain. I fully intended returning when the time came. I did not seek to escape my share of responsibility. But Fate was trailing me, sifting through his bag of tricks to see which prank would best suit the moment.

Whether my appearance at that time was merely fortuitous, I do not know. It is possible that any child would have served his purpose. But that I, the Moor's 'special friend,' should be the one, that was a far finer rebuke to the Inquisitor, indeed the entire community, compromised as they were by accusation and testimony.

A rough hand clamped itself over my mouth. I grasped the hand, which smelled of unwashed wool, but it was tightly pressed about my face, while a second hand had me by the hair, the arm curled round my neck. The speed and unexpectedness of the assault were the most immediately frightening thing. I did not at that moment actually think someone was trying to kill me; but everything being so abrupt, that I found terrifying.

I kicked and screamed, but my blows had no impact on the sturdy legs behind me, and the hand ensured that my screams were stifled. I was being manhandled into an orchard a little way from the Two Sisters path. My attacker bundled me over a wall, at precisely that point, I noted, where a red cross was daubed on the stone. The fact seems irrelevant now, but at the time the red cross struck me as being a very particular and very personal message.

Beyond the wall, the hand was withdrawn from my face, but the moment I opened my mouth to cry out, I was gagged by a rough wadding of hessian. Then a length of coarse raw silk was rapidly, expertly wound round my head, at once blindfolding and muzzling me. My hands and ankles were bound as quickly. A blow to the back of the knees buckled my legs while a sack was pulled over my head and fastened about my feet. I believe throughout this I still fought, but the thrashings of terror are so spastic I do not know if I landed a blow or in any wise improved my chances of escape.

I was then dragged a little way before being strapped to the back of a beast of burden, a mule

I guessed, judging by the way my attacker grunted as he hefted me high over the animal's shoulders. Trussed to the back of the beast, I was taken I knew not where, but up somewhere, away from the *aldea*, up into the mountain, the mule's hooves occasionally squelching through mud as we climbed alongside a chattering stream. There was no telling what stream, no knowing where I was going, and no resisting the going there. Eventually, I realized my struggles were fruitless, and just lay there, slung over the back of the mule.

At length, the rope binding the ends of the sack below the belly of the mule was cut and I was pulled to the ground, dumped with as much ceremony as a sack of grain. A door opened and I was hauled inside. It was dry and cool and when the sack was opened I noticed a familiar odor of corruption.

Then my panicked heart stopped its frantic beating, stilled by an even greater terror, a horror so deep it made the preceding minutes seem the merest jest. I knew where I was. I was in the Factor's cave. And those rough, wool-scented hands belonged to the Factor.

A peck here, a peck there.

* * *

The intensity of my horror may seem unusually prescient. You may protest that a known assailant is less terrible than an unknown, that a recognizable location is less terrifying than ignorance, but that underestimates the impact on a childish mind of repeated warnings to stay away from a particular individual. That character becomes one with all the phantoms and terrors an imaginative child can conjure, becomes in some manner cloaked with a poorly perceived but pervasive sense of evil. And if fancy lacked conviction, I had already taken my first faltering steps toward a more specific knowledge of evil. I had visited the Factor's cave once before. I had penetrated the darkness, groping my way along that strangely tactile wall, breathing deep of the fetid air. I had touched the long soft cobweb, stumbled on the woodpile, had heard the groan—would that I had been spared that sound, it haunts me still, still I try to interpret it as something other than the last prolonged suffering of another child. Perhaps, in the furthest recesses of my heart, I had known from the start what these things were, had known the 'cobweb' was no cobweb, the 'woodpile' no woodpile, but had not been prepared to surrender the comforting falsehoods of rationalization.

The door safely fastened, I was taken from my sack and hung against the wall by a hook thrust through the loose weave of my shirt, my toes just touching the ground. My hands were still tied behind my back, my feet were still bound, my mouth still gagged, but the bandage about my eyes was tugged down so that I could see.

The Factor turned his back on me, turned to deal with his other victim, for as I hung there, peering into the patchy dark of the unlit cave, his lamb came nuzzling about his legs, butting the man's knees as if searching for milk. For all the petting and care lavished on this creature in the preceding weeks, its end was unceremonious. The Factor bent down, grasped its legs and upturned it on the rough table, the head hanging over the deeply scoured end. Discomfited, the lamb struggled a little, but the Factor held it still. A knife appeared and was placed against the lamb's throat. With a quick, practiced movement, the Factor pierced his mascot's carotid artery. The lamb kicked awhile, then its eyes glazed and it shuddered as the blood dripped into a basin placed below the table.

When the lamb was bled, the Factor took the brimming basin and a stick with a length of sack-cloth wrapped round its head. Dipping the stick in the basin, he began to daub the dark walls with blood. His work was hampered by lack of light, so he approached the wall at the mouth of the cave, where a few embers of the fire on which he cooked his food still glowed faintly. Taking a taper from a crack in the wall, he held it to the cinders till it caught, then placed it in a shallow dish of oil.

As he moved back to his basin, I could see in the feeble flickering light of the taper, the 'mineral deposit' I had felt under my fingers during my previous visit. The walls of the cave were washed with blood, most of it blackened by time, but with a few patches retaining a ruddy hue. All but the most recently painted sections were dry and powdery.

Once the basin was empty, the lamb's forelegs were tied together and the carcass was suspended from a hook set in a strut bridging the table. He slit the belly of the beast and plunged his hands inside to scoop out the entrails, which were deposited in the same basin, where they settled slowly, steaming lightly. Unhooking the eviscerated lamb, he transferred the slip knot from the fore to the hind legs, then hung the carcass head down. Nicking the skin about the beast's ankles, he sliced along the inside of its hind legs. After working the legs free of the skin, he grasped the hide about the anus and, grunting with exertion, stripped the fleece, occasionally employing the knife when the skin stuck

too closely to the meat. He then lowered the carcass and started working round the joints of the
legs, levering apart the sinews with the short, sharp
blade of his knife.

And throughout the butchery, he maintained a
running commentary, describing what he was doing
and how he would afterwards prepare each cut.
Every now and again, he would point out the dif-
ferences between butchering a lamb and a human
being. For that was clearly what he intended. The
lamb came first, but soon I would have that same
knife at my throat, my blood would adorn the
walls, my entrails would mix with the lamb's, I
would be stripped of my skin, my sinews would be
cracked apart. . . .

"When a creature grows large and ugly," he
explained, working methodically, "when its pret-
tiness is past, it is a kindness to kill it. We cannot
let what is young and pretty decay. We must save
it from attrition and take it into ourselves. These
tendons here, it's the Devil's own job to cut them.
They're easier in a child, snap away quite cleanly,
but in these awkward beasts, no; it's a mercy when
you save a creature from growing old. Of course,
some of them are scarcely worth the saving. Great
loutish ugly lads. Coarse grained, like I say. Them
I don't help at all. Too heavy on the stomach. Them

I leave to make their own transition. The question is, what shall we do with you, my pretty? Should we keep you here, make a feast of it in the cave, or are you better suited to the pit?" He paused in his butchery and looked at me, as if my terrified eyes might hold the answer. "You understand which pit I mean? Below the Shepherd's Leap there. Where you boys tip the rocks over. I've left two of your kind there. In the shallow pit. Ugly boys with poor meat on them. It was all they were good for."

At this I retched and hot vomit rushed into my throat. I do not know what horrified me more. That this man was apparently confessing to eating the flesh of those he butchered or the realization that he had also left children in the pits below the Shepherd's Leap, that there had perhaps been a living child down there when we tossed rocks over the edge for the thrill of hearing nothing. I think perhaps the second was the worst. For any gagged and bound child down there would have heard our voices, would have known what was coming. I choked on the vomit and would have died had the Factor not pulled down my gag and extracted the rag from my mouth. He had no need to fear I would give him away now. I was dumbstruck with horror and, even had I been able to cry out, everyone was at the execution. The vomit spilled onto the floor.

"Perhaps we will keep you here awhile," he said, once my gasping had subsided. "You have a hint of innocence about you yet. And it will better please me to know that I have you here when the Moor is dead. That will teach him. He'll not humiliate me again. When he knows he's executed a man for murder, but the murder hasn't stopped."

I do not know what prompted the other disappearances. The Factor had some sick notion about beauty and innocence and sacrifice, that much I understand; but by what device did he determine the kidnapping of a child? Was it a kind of hunger that became unappeasable after awhile? Was he influenced by the phases of the moon? Did he function by the seasons or have a calendar of his own making with high days and holy days demanding some special observation? Or did he simply take a child when chance presented itself? I cannot say, but in my case, the motive was clear. He wanted to revenge himself on the Inquisitor for that public humiliation. Let the Inquisitor do his work, then find it all undone by another child gone on the very day the Moor was executed for the crime.

"You'll not want for company," said the Factor, taking his tiny flickering lamp and striding down the narrowing cave. Twisting my neck, I could just make out my 'cobweb,' the long hair hanging from a head, a human head, suspended from the roof of the cave. The face was small, dark, wrinkled, smoked with a process of aging it had never known in life. The Factor kicked at something on the ground. There was a clatter, dry and brittle. There was no pretending it was a pile of wood.

Even then, in my own dire predicament, I endeavored to persuade myself I had not heard the groan when I first went to the cave. I could accept the bones, even the head, but the thought that the last child, who had disappeared two months earlier, might still have been alive at that time, was too strong for me.

The Factor returned to the table and, after a few practiced incisions, extracted the long strong tongue from his former pet.

* * *

Doubtless you read of this with horror. You consider this man a beast, an evil being, a monster capable of deeds no right-thinking man could contemplate. Would that it were so. We all want to ascribe grotesque deeds to an inhuman agent, but the business of blood and its shedding is an all too human affair. Take any nation in any generation and you will find there is no shortage of healthy men and women

willing to experiment with murder and torture.
Look to yourselves, my lords, look to the institu-
tion you represent, and the crimes it has committed
these last two centuries. I grant you, you never lay
hands on your victims yourselves. All you touch is
your portion of the lucre they pay for the privilege
of being denounced and murdered. You have the
civil authorities do the bodily work for you. But the
experiment is yours. You institute proceedings, you
call for the hard ordeal, you sanction the act with
your supple piety. Do not condemn the Factor. He
was no monster, but a man, a man not unlike yourselves. Again, take any nation in any generation
and you will find people ready to shed blood for
an idea, ready indeed to define an idea by the shedding of blood. And these people will always prey
on those willing to experiment with murder and
torture, fashioning a framework in which the idea
may be served by the desire to do harm. The Factor's only peculiarity was that he was at once the
man with the idea and the executioner.

The Inquisitor and I spoke of these events only
once, many years later, shortly before he himself
was arrested. He confirmed the political mission he
had undertaken, his understanding that the Moor's
life was a necessary sacrifice to the still fragile community, the necessity of unanimity and my own

participation. At the time, such acts were taking place all over the South, minor spectacles of politicking, manipulating circumstances on the ground to make the people feel the ground was theirs. These things he confirmed. But there was one thing he did not explain, even obliquely, and it was only later, when I returned to the mountain, that I was able to verify my conjecture. He did not speak of what happened after the execution. He did not say why his feet were wet.

At the time of our last interview, he was about to be arraigned as a sympathizer of the *alumbrados*. That was fitting in light of what he did on the day of the execution. It was, you see, the self-same search for reason, which later led him to heresy, that motivated his actions after the Moor's death. He was a man who had to explain things to himself, even petty phenomena with no impact on his political work or spiritual progress. He was in some ways closer to the Moor than one might at first suppose. The one sought to explain the world through reason, the other through stories, but they were both elucidators, endeavoring to clarify through narrative. It was perhaps that quest for clarity that had originally irritated the resentment of my people, for when one lives in darkness, the light shining in the house of one's neighbor is a bound-less provocation. By the end of his life, the Inquis-itor had himself learned the danger of clarity: clarity exposes the dark corners in which gentlemen like you reside, my lords, clarity illuminates the flaws in your scheme of things, clarity is the handmaiden of liberty, and is never favored by precarious power. Clarity is at once the goad of the weak and the enemy of authority.

I suspect that is also why the Factor never reani-mated the fire in all the hours I was his captive. The cave was terribly dark and his butchery cannot have been made easier by the gloom, but he restricted himself to that one weak taper dipped in oil. As I have observed before, he was a poor, weak creature himself, and probably knew it. Hence the pleasure of exercising power over others. Be it tenants in arrears or youth about to lose its bloom, he profited from situations in which he enjoyed control. Any more light in his cave and his weakness would have been exposed. Obscurity was his power.

I was by now keenly aware that the dismember-ment of the lamb was drawing to a close. The legs were hung by thongs of twine from the roof of the cave, the offal had been sorted and cleaned, the chops cracked apart, the bloody head dumped in an iron pot, the spine stripped of its cord and cut into segments. It would be my turn next. Yet immobilized as I was, my collar pierced by the hook protruding from the wall, there was nothing I could do. All I had was my tongue and, judging by the business with the lamb, I wouldn't be keeping that much longer. I had to make best use of it while I could.

"They'll be looking for me," I said, hesitantly, half fearing he would beat me into silence, or gag me, or worse still start with the knife. But, instead, he smiled at me.

I have already spoken of that smile. You may well imagine how much more horrible it was to me in the predicament in which I then found myself. With the Factor's forearms all smeared with blood almost to the elbows and the carnage scattered about the cave, his smile resembled a hungry wound. And yet, there was a kind of empathy in his expression, too. It is not my intention to evoke sympathy for the killer. This man had done terrible deeds and, though there was a strange reason in his madness, as there is behind all man's folly, he was not deserving of sympathy. But in that moment, I believe he felt a genuine pity for my naiveté. It was a comparable pity, perhaps, that moved him to his various murders. Butchering what he perceived to be innocence, he was in his own way preserving it from disappointment and betrayal.

"That's what they all say," he said, softly, with chilling compassion.

Doubtless it was true. Every child he killed had probably entertained some wild hope of rescue. And though my own words were also true, they would be looking for me, eventually, I knew how fruitless such searches had been in the past. Nothing was ever found. The children simply disappeared. My own case was especially hopeless. Amid the crowds, my absence would not be noted soon, and were it so, there was reason enough to suppose I had taken myself elsewhere. I was, after all, the Moor's special friend. It was known that I went on solitary walks in the mountains. And it was only natural that I should have removed myself from the scene of my friend's execution. But in that lay my hope, too. I did not as yet see how I could exploit the circumstance, but I had understood something of the commentary during the lamb's butchering, had perceived that my disappearance was intended in part at least as a rebuke to the Inquisitor, a sign that he had executed the wrong man.

"They'll think I've run away," I said. "They'll think I've gone because of what they did to the Moor." At first, the Factor did not grasp the implication of this. He merely shrugged, as if it were a matter of no importance. But then he paused,

stilled by a sudden understanding, and looked
at me closely. Encouraged, I continued speaking.
"They won't know I'm killed. So they won't know
it wasn't the Moor killed the other children. They
won't know they've executed the wrong man, that
the Inquisitor got it wrong."

As I say, I did not at the time know where this
was leading, but I sensed it was my only hope, to
point out the defect in his plan for revenge. Clearly
the Factor was now fully aware of this flaw, for
he sat heavily on a stool, his smile replaced by an
expression of pained frustration, like a child himself contemplating some monstrous and unmerited
injury. At length, though, he seemed to see a way
out of his difficulty.

"That's all right," he said, smiling again. "I'll
give them a piece of you. Several pieces perhaps.
A foot here, a finger there. Some flesh in the bucket
of the well. Or the head, that would be good. They
won't believe you've run away without your feet,
will they now? Nor headless, I'd warrant."

His logic, within the constraints of his madness,
was sound, forcing me to think fast. In retrospect,
the Factor's desire to murder me was perhaps the
most inspiring lesson in dialectic I ever received.
The Jesuits taught me rhetoric, told countless lessons in reason and debate, but their sanctions were

never so compelling as the Factor's, and what his teaching lacked in method it compensated for with motive. I assure you, it concentrates the mind most wonderfully when the matter of debate is the degree to which one's own body is to be dismembered. But that is a lesson you do not need me to teach you.

"But if you give them all of me," I said, hurriedly, "all of me, alive, I mean. Then they won't be able to forget. They'll see me every day. And everytime they see me, they'll remember that they got it wrong."

"Give them all of you? And let you talk? You must think I'm stupid."

I had anticipated this. But I had also watched him butcher the lamb. I had seen that dexterous excision. A living rebuke had to be better than a fading memory.

"Nearly all of me," I said. "Put out my eyes, cut out my tongue. I can show them nothing, tell them nothing, but they'll still know." It was, of course, an appalling risk to take. He might as easily have kept me there, mutilating me in the cave and waiting till my wounds had healed before leaving me in the village. But it was the only chance I could see of getting some measure of freedom. "But it must be done now," I added. "Straight away. While the crowds are still there. They must see me arrive, walking in with my wounds. Then they'll know. Everyone will know. Everyone."

Walk on, bright boy, walk on!

* * *

I could not, of course, know the help I would receive. One never does. But my reasoning proved inspired. A more spectacular rebuke of the Inquisitor could not be imagined. Nothing would give the lie to his stage trial so well as such vivid evidence, walking into the *aldea* at the very moment when his work was thought to be concluded. And for it to be most effective, I had to be capable of walking by myself. Which meant the maiming could not take place till we were near the *aldea*.

I could see the Factor calculating the odds. He must have known the risk he was taking. I daren't point out the necessary delay to my wounding for fear he would suspect I had a plan, which in truth I did not. But the living, bleeding rebuke, that held too strong an appeal to resist. As it happened, my escape came sooner than I had anticipated or, indeed, really desired, for the occasion, though initially masked by a more desperate impression, presented itself almost immediately.

The Factor stood and came towards me. His left hand reached behind me, his right rose from his belt, and in it he held the knife he'd used to butcher the lamb, its blade spattered with the glutinous thread of the spinal column and specks of bloodied flesh drying to gore. For a moment, I thought all my arguments had been in vain. I had no time to scream. A dead, cold hand clasped my heart. I almost sensed the kiss of his blade, the prick of its tongue piercing my throat, seeking out the artery. But I had mistaken his intentions, for all he did was spread the cloth of my shirt with his left hand and cut the material with his right, so that I dropped the small distance to the floor. At first my legs gave way and I began to slide down the wall, but my descent was checked by the Factor's hand, cupped under my chin, the forefinger and thumb splayed across my throat, like a rude crutch supporting the over heavy bough of a laden fruit tree.

"This is how it will be," he said. "We follow the stream down to the Pozo de los Muchachos, you understand?" I did. He was referring to a large pool where we children occasionally bathed in the summer. It was otherwise an obscure corner and there was little chance we would meet anyone en route. "Then we climb round the *solana*, to the *humilladero*. And there we do the business."

He was evidently nervous, but it was, in the circumstances, a relatively well thought out plan. There were no major paths or trails to the south of the *aldea*, as all direct routes that way ended on a precipitous escarpment, while the shrine he mentioned was so small it could scarcely hope to attract any devotees on a day like this, when better entertainment was to be had in the plaza. The risk was still real, far greater than simply dispensing with me in his cave, but the reward of the Inquisitor's public humiliation was correspondingly greater. Curiously, the way he spoke of 'the business,' it seemed as if the Factor felt we were conspiring in this matter, as if blinding me and cutting out my tongue were some jape we had conjured between us. Perhaps he was right.

If evidence of his nervousness were required, it lay in his subsequent negligence, for when he opened the door to ensure there were no onlookers, he forgot to re-tie my blindfold. Satisfied that all was clear, he motioned me forward. I hobbled across the rough floor of the cave, my hands and feet still bound. But the moment I emerged blinking into the bright light, he shoved me back with a curse. In his haste to get me inside the cave, he had failed to tether his mule and, though the animal had not wandered far (even I, dazzled though I was, had glimpsed it a little way down the stream), it still had to be fetched.

The door was secured again. This, I realized, was my chance. It was not the best moment to try and escape. I was far from help, at the head of an impasse, with the Factor between me and the mouth of the valley. But that I had survived thus far already seemed so highly improbable that I was prepared to grasp any opportunity, no matter how slender, how doubtful of success. I had first to free myself of my bonds. I cast about for some tool with which to effect this, but the Factor had tucked his knife back into his belt and the table, though rough, was scarcely an appropriate instrument for abrading a rope in the time available. I briefly thought of the bones upon which I had stumbled in my earlier visit, but they were too far, and I could not in any case countenance running into that awful hanging head. Then I saw the taper. It was still burning, weakly, but burning nonetheless.

My hands were numb from their long immobilization, but I could feel the heat as I positioned myself and sought to place the rope above the flame. The smell of burning hemp mixed with the sweet scent of scorched skin, confirming that my blind groping had located its target. The pain rapidly became acute, but I stuck to it until I heard the clatter of the mule's hooves, perhaps some thirty or forty steps from the cave's entrance. I had no more time. The Factor was coming. He would smell the rope, the skin, know something was amiss. I tried to pull the rope apart, but it still dug into my wrists without rending.

The mule's hooves sounded clearer and I could hear the Factor humming to himself, making a thin, whining noise akin to a sustained sob. Then I spotted the iron pot containing the lamb's head. I shuffled over and began chafing the scorched rope against its rim.

The mule was at the door, and the Factor was tethering the creature against a hook in the wall, still whining to himself, the sound pitched at a level suggesting barely suppressed panic. I had to escape before he lost his nerve altogether and elected a less audacious method of disposing of me. The rope sundered and I nearly fell, making the pot rattle before I regained my feet. I stood still in an agony of expectation, but it seemed the Factor had not heard me. He would be turning toward the door, though. He'd be coming in at any moment. I untied the knot at my feet and stepped onto the shallow concave rock beside the wall where he built his fire.

My weight displaced the ashes of the fire and hot hidden cinders burned the soles of my feet, but I had little concern for that, for the door had been lifted slightly so it would swing more easily. The Factor was about to discover my flight. The instant he came through the doorway, I slipped through the smoke vent in the wall, just as I had done twice before.

It must have taken his eyes a moment to accustom themselves to the dark, because he did not cry out at once, and in the seconds it took him to discover my departure, I made a calculation more rapid than anything the Jesuits ever extracted from me. I had three options. I could drop directly off the wall and endeavor to outrun the Factor in a straight race down the stream. I could descend, untie the mule, and ride to safety. Or I could climb the cliff and join the Acequia Nueva beyond the Shepherd's Leap. The mule was obviously the surest way of escaping if I got it loose in time, but that 'if' was the rub, for were the Factor to emerge before I was astride the beast and on my way, I would be lost. I could probably run faster than him, but the streambed option would be fatal if he had sense enough to mount the mule. My best hope, it seemed, was to climb. I was no climber, but I was lighter and more nimble than the Factor, and would to some degree benefit from my superior agility.

There was a narrow shelf where the stones of the rough wall met the overhanging rock and I was already edging my way along this toward the cliff when the Factor came plunging from the cave, bawling dismay. The mule, frightened by the sudden excursion, pulled back in alarm, stamping at the ground and pulling on its tether, and in the subsequent confusion, I was able to progress a good two thirds of the way along the wall before the Factor saw me.

He jumped, snatching at my legs.

The first time he nearly had me. I felt his nails scrape across my ankle. But failing to catch me, his panic got the better of him, and his second leap was way off mark.

At the time, all my energies were concentrated on keeping my feet clear of his scrabbling hands, but I can still picture him clutching at me, and though the image excites all the old horror, it is faintly comical as well. In his desperate eagerness, the Factor was not thinking clearly, and rather than climbing the wall or carefully aiming his attempts to catch me, he was leaping wildly and grasping at empty space, like a lunatic tormented by imaginary bees, or some savage beast teased by a beauty beyond its understanding, say an ape listening to music. The mysterious sounds were all about him, but he could not seize them and, taunted beyond reason, he lunged blindly, grappling at thin air, as if he could capture the music of the spheres.

This image, my lords, is not idle fancy. I suspect that is how the Factor was in life, too. Aware that there was something beautiful in youth and vitality, but unable to know what it was, he sought to capture it by dismembering it, like one of those surgeons digging about in corpses in search of the soul, unmindful of the fact that in digging they destroy what they seek. Such fallacies, my lords, may even be encountered in our own church. There are many men in Christendom, my lords, who are dimly aware that in religion there lies a reflection of God's glory, a means of inspiring and channeling what is finest in mankind, and a manifest for celebrating everything that makes life worth living. Yet these men, my lords, do not understand its essential fluidity, that this glory and celebration cannot be set in a rigid code that can be recited and tinkered with and imposed on others, but that it comes from within and from being at one with God and the world. Such men, my lords, subsist on dogma and the dismal imbecilities of those who would codify life, snatching aimlessly at a beauty they do not understand and can never comprehend.

At length, the Factor realized he would never catch me in this manner. He dropped to the ground and fetched up a stone. Intending to dislodge me from my perch, he began pelting me with small rocks and handfuls of gravel. By this time though, I was at the end of the wall and beginning my precarious ascent of the cliff.

It was not an exceptionally steep cliff. A fall would have been fatal, even in normal circumstances, but as cliffs go, it was relatively shallow, almost a very steep slope rather than a cliff. Unfortunately, despite the scorching they'd received, my feet and hands were still numb from the tight bonds. Unable to rely upon touch alone, I had to look to every move I made, willing my fingers to hold a stone, forcing my toes to find purchase in crevices and on ledges. Even then, I slipped several times, tearing my nails and barking the thin skin on my knuckles and shins as I struggled to recover some grip or small foothold. The easiest stretches were those where I could scramble on all fours like a dog, but these were easier for the Factor, too.

With an unearthly roar of rage, he had flung himself at the cliff and was climbing behind me. He was a heavy man, unused to anything more acrobatic than the mental gymnastic of his tally

stick, but I was made clumsy by my numb extremi-
ties and I doubt an impartial observer would have
cared to call the race one way or the other. As for
incentive, we were equally matched, for we were
both climbing for our lives, the Factor knowing full
well that were I to escape, his tenure on the world
was forfeit. The only real advantage I had was the
distance I had climbed before he began his pursuit.

I could hear his heavy breathing behind me, the
fall of rock as he scrambled over loose scree, the
scrabbling of his hands, and the occasional grunts
to which his shouts were soon reduced.

And the higher we climbed, the closer he seemed.

It sounded like he was sobbing at one point. Not
weeping, but whimpering with a desperate passion,
cadenced as much by desolation and desire as exertion. It was worse than the grunting because more
keenly pitched, so that I had the feeling he was
right behind me, would soon be breathing in my
ear, slobbering shrill cries of inexplicable need.

And closer all the time, closer and closer and closer.

Toward the top, I risked a glance over my shoulder.

My vision swam, exhaustion and fear combining
with the dizzying drop to rob me of balance, and I
nearly fell. Again, as with every hand and toe hold,
it was only an effort of will that mastered my physical senses, for by then my body was screaming for

rest and would, left to its own devices, have gladly
dropped from the cliff to gain a momentary respite.
To lie still for a few seconds, that was all it asked,
but I knew that a few seconds would run to eternity
in the present circumstances.

The Factor was still the length of two men
behind me, but he seemed to have gained energy,
was moving more quickly, for he saw the top was
near and was perhaps persuaded that there he
would catch me. His face gleamed with sweat and
his anxious upturned eyes seemed to be pleading
with me, as if he rather than I were the victim.

For my part, I was equally sure, or almost sure,
that I could escape him, once past the lip of the cliff.
The only question was which way to go. If I headed
up the mountain, I would have the advantage, for
I knew the terrain and was fitter than the Factor.
But climbing would mean distancing myself from
help, would mean an awful fraught night, hiding
and running, hoping the dark did not conceal the
waiting hunter. Thus it was that, when I reached the
path, I turned toward the Shepherd's Leap, for that
way lay the *aldea* and help.

The Factor reached the path shortly after me and
cried out again, this time in triumph, for he must
have thought that running downhill he was sure

to catch me. Maybe he would have. Maybe I had made the wrong choice. I cannot say. Because as I rounded the curve above the smaller cliff and came to the fearful drop above the Shepherd's Leap, I almost collided with the Inquisitor.

"What in God's name!" he cried. "What were those screams and roars? I. . . ."

The Factor came careering round the corner and stopped abruptly a few strides short of where we stood.

"It's him," I shouted, slipping behind the shield of the Inquisitor's body. "He's the one that did it. He's the killer. Not the Moor. In his cave. He's got bones and heads. He killed the children."

The accusation was never debated. The two men looked at one another. Perhaps both understood the pass to which they had come. The Factor had no choice. Both the Inquisitor and I had to die if he was to live. He dashed at us, leaning into the charge, a rising cry of battle breaking from his lips.

I know little of the Inquisitor's background. Though he was my mentor and unseen protector for many years, he was a very private man and did not speak much of his past, of where he came from, what class of learning he had known, whether he had been trained in warfare or experienced fighting for himself. But he was quick and cunning, knew something of how to parry an opponent and use the greater weight of an enemy to his own advantage.

As the Factor hurtled toward us, his stocky legs barely keeping pace with the precipitate rush of his bulky body, the Inquisitor ducked, not from the waist but bending his knees, so that when the impact came, he was already pushing up and forward, catching the Factor's belly with his shoulder, cutting short the battle cry. He continued to rise, seemingly higher than his natural height allowed, lifting his shoulder and simultaneously raising the elbow below it, springing from the legs all the while, so that the Factor was pitched into air, as if tossed by a bull. Carried forth by his own momentum, the Factor flipped over the Inquisitor's head and sailed through the air, slipping over the edge of the Shepherd's Leap.

He never made a sound. He did not scream or shout or protest in any way. I saw his face briefly as he passed. It looked stunned, perhaps a little aggrieved, even pathetic, comical in any other circumstances, but there seemed to be no foreknowledge of death, no sense of impending doom, no fear of eternal damnation. Then he disappeared from sight, plunging into his long silent fall. For not only was there no scream, there was no sound of his landing, either. That was the eerie part. It was as if he just kept falling for ever and ever, tumbling through the air into nothingness. I know he must have fallen into one of the snow-holes, must have gone deep into the ground where the thud of his landing was muffled, but in my mind he is there still, falling through the air for all eternity.

You will perhaps be familiar with the way the Inquisitor met his end. I was not there, but I heard tell of his dignity, of how he refused to beg for your false and uncertain mercy, and did not cry out during his sufferings. He was equally imperturbable at the Shepherd's Leap. He straightened his clothing, brushed a fleck of dust-encrusted meat from his shoulder, and turned to me, his hard dark eyes boring into my own.

"It is done," he said.

I knew he was not talking about the Factor. It was the Moor he meant. And with that, overwhelmed by grief and exhaustion and fear, I subsided to the ground, too tired to weep but so full of sorrow I wanted to stay in that place for ever after and never move again. Perhaps that's what happened. Oftentimes I feel that, for all my travels, the most vital part of me was left behind on the mountain. It was then, lying on the edge of the Shepherd's Leap, that I noticed the Inquisitor's feet were wet, his leather slippers splashed with a dark line of water that stopped just short of the stitching round the upper seam.

* * *

My story is told. You may come for me, my lords, read my manuscript, make of it what you will, and burn it as you will my body. You may find it strange that a man of my years faced with a disagreeable death should spend his last days recalling his childhood, but the repetition of rules and the rote learning of ritual's dull formulae are not the only functions of memory. Reminiscence is more vital than regulation or prescription; it is the process by which we tease out the thread of meaning, and as such is a fitting pursuit for a man confronting mortality.

In age, my lords, we return to the lessons of our youth. Indeed, it is only then that we understand them. Telling tales of our childhood, we learn what we were, what we have been, and what we have become, the first in the events, the second in the telling, the third in the value we ascribe to those events. And by relating the Moor's history, I pay tribute to the magic and mystery he embodied. That is the ultimate purpose of all stories, to evoke the heartbreaking enchantments of childhood, reviving that half-forgotten intensity of feeling, and remind ourselves of a time when the world was a thing of wonder and a thing of terror.

You will not understand this. I spoke earlier of the book by Ibn Tufayl. His bright boy learned that there are three categories of men: those who understand truth by reason alone, those who understand by the symbols of revelation, and those who accept the laws that derive from symbols of revelation. I would add to that, those who understand through the telling of stories, which are in their own way a symbol of revelation, and those who understand nothing for they are blinded by laws that define the shape of inner truth without clarifying its nature. Now, since you, my lords, are proving tardy (perhaps nearsightedness has obscured your way?), I will refer you to the subject of another tale from the Moor's repertory.

He told me once of the Garden of Irem, a kind of Mohammedan Babylon, a place so beautiful it amounted to an act of hubris and was therefore destroyed by God, only to be seen thereafter in

ephemeral glimpses, manifesting itself to the occasional lone traveler before fading away again and
disappearing in the wastes of the desert. This is the
matter of all our lives, my lords; we are all of us
trying to catch a glimpse of that garden, and I was
granted such a favor through the eyes of the Moor.
Looking back now, I think I learned no wisdom
from the Moor. I do not know what wisdom is.
But he taught me to look, to see the fleeting paradise that can materialize on earth, taught me a taste
for life when everyone else loved death. And that,
my lords, is the great weakness of our religion. In
seeking to disarm it, we have made a cult of death,
and so have lost the capacity to conjure our own
half-remembered garden. As a result, the death
lovers come to their end full of regret, for they have
embraced death when they should have lived and
cannot live now that they die. Only those who learn
a taste for life, who glimpse the Garden of Irem, lose
their fear of death, for they have touched the truth
of being and can relinquish life with ease, comforted by the knowledge that they have lived large
and wide and well. I am ready to die, my lords.

The Inquisitor was ruthlessly efficient in resolving
the business of the Factor. He had the cave sealed
and forbad anyone to go into that place, and I do

not believe anyone ever did. Fifteen years later, there was an earthquake in the mountain, the cave collapsed, and its former entrance is now nothing but a slope of rubble. As for myself, I was spirited off by the Inquisitor's clerk, sent directly to my education in order to prevent my telling what I knew and thus undoing the work he had done to make of guilt and fear a mortar that would bind our fragile community together. I did not mind being sent away. My family and fellow villagers had all become strangers to me. My only regret at that time was that I had missed the Moor's execution, for I had fully intended returning to witness the deed for myself.

I had no wish to see him die, but I understood that if you will not or cannot act to prevent something happening, you must be prepared to look at the consequences of your inaction. The regret and its attendant guilt have adhered to me ever since. At first, my remorse was so intense it seemed like a curse. A child cannot know what to do with a load of guilt like that and I could not confess to the church for it was the church that had occasioned my sin. So I had to carry it. But that, I came to realize, was no bad thing. For it is only in carrying sin that we become human, by knowing the weight of what we have done or should have done and did not, knowing what we are doing and should be doing but are not. Christ was born in order to take on the burden of man's sin, but we are made human by knowing that burden for ourselves, and it is as well to remind ourselves of it once in a while. I was glad to know the guilt. Now, though, the end is near and it is time to divest myself of these worldly encumbrances.

In my last meeting with the Inquisitor many years later, I asked him again about those events. He was, understandably enough, not keen to talk of them, but he realized he owed me a repeated explanation. Was the Moor's death really necessary? Could propaganda not have done as well? Could we not have defined ourselves against the English or the Dutch or the French? He admitted that perhaps we could, but an enemy faith, he said, is always a better foe than an enemy nation because it is more nebulous, more tractable, more menacing. 'They' can be anywhere, their insidious influence interpreted in any mishap, and the fact that we cannot see them only confirms their devious ubiquity. At the end of his life, I believe the Inquisitor regretted his political compromises. He had, at best, been doing the Devil's work on behalf of

God. At worst, God had been suborned by the
Devil. It was not a job he could recollect with any
satisfaction. And he knew by then that any entity
relying upon an enemy for the definition of self, is
fatally flawed.

Our country, my lords, will not become a
coherent nation till it is sufficiently sure of itself to
forget the need of an enemy. Just so, our church will
never recover its original purity of purpose and tol-
erance till it has no need of people like you, men so
jealous and uncertain in their own faith that they
must expose the failure of everyone else's. And this
holds true for individuals, too. No man has become
himself until he is confident enough not to define
himself in opposition to others. So long as you hold
yourself high by trimming another's talents, so long
as you feed on the sour fruits of blame and drink at
the fountain of censure, so long as you hobble along
on crutches of scorn and exclusion, you are nothing
but a scrap of flesh animated by a craving for a conviction you do not merit and an ascendancy you do
not deserve.

I suppose there will always be people like you,
my lords, people who want the courage to face
their God but must define Him and themselves by
the making of external enemies, people for whom
what they are can only be affirmed by declaring

what they are not, who fear life and the complexities of being and must reduce everything to the banality of their own poor comprehension. Perhaps this is because when we reduce things they become more piquant and can be tasted by a blunted palate. I do not know. You, my lords, are better placed to judge.

But there will always be people like the Moor, too, who will counter your deadening influence. Men like you win many victories, maybe most, but you will never defeat men like him, not in the end, for the shadows of men like the Moor are long and their passing leaves a lasting mark on the ground. Their tread falls softly, *ship-ship*, but the footsteps are there for those with eyes to see, and no matter how hard you huff and you puff, my lords, you cannot blow away every sign they make. Some trails persist as a mere scattering of footprints in the sand, others become broad thoroughfares thronged by a clattering concord of human-being, but no matter how faint it may be, every path taken by people in the past can be traced in the present, informing likeminded men as they map their own way through world.

Come, my lords, kill me if you wish, burn these poor papers, foreswear the Moor's heritage: it will change nothing, for we will still be here, will always stand against you in one guise or another. You cannot kill us all, you cannot burn every book, unravel every story, erase every memory. Your paltry weapons are as nothing to the power of the human heart and the will to reason. I have made my confession. Let it be.

I only returned to the *aldea* once. It was some years after the Inquisitor had met the same fate as the Moor, condemned according to kind by his own judgment. I spoke to no one, told my retinue to ensure no one spoke to me, and walked alone in the mountain; up past the fields with their dry stone walls still daubed with crosses, up past the Shepherd's Leap and along the Acequia Nueva, to the place where the Moor had walked on water, where I divined the Inquisitor had wet his feet after the execution in order to test the miracle for himself, and from where he had been returning when the Factor and I caught up with him.

It took me a while to find it, but I eventually discovered the spot. Running along the center of the *acequia*, midway between the two walls, flush with the water level, there lies a thin blade of rock, so pale and fine it is virtually invisible in the bubbling stream. I was already grown old, had lost my former agility, but despite my ungainliness, I found that it was possible, with a little care, to do as the Moor had done and the Inquisitor after him.

Balancing on the scarcely perceptible line of rock, my arms outstretched, weeping for all that was lost and all that was gained, laughing at my temerity and ludicrous tottering progress, I followed in the footsteps of greater men than me, and I walked on water.

I walked on water, my lords.

I walked on water!

This is the trick of life. You take what it gives you and turn it to magic. A blade of rock plated with the silvery waters of a mountain spring is the making of a miracle at which children may marvel; a story poorly lived but well told generates a reality truer than itself that aspires to a kind of immortality; a lunatic crying in the wilderness can shout loud enough to found a religion that will echo down the ages. This magic is the gift of dreams. It does not matter what you dream. Whether you make a dream for yourself alone or one that would encompass all humanity, is of no account. But dream you must, because if you choose an existence that lacks illusion and does not convert the clod of being to a thing of wonder and celebration, then you will die before ever you have lived, and your time in this world will have been no better than a guttering candle roughly fashioned of cheap tallow.

Walk on, bright boy, walk on.

* * *